A WYATT BOOK *for*

W

— ST. —
MARTIN'S
P R E S S

MICHAEL KING

Lorien Lost

A Wyatt Book *for*

St. Martin's Press ❧ New York

Acknowledgments appear on pages 193-195.

Edited and designed by Iris Bass
Typography by Songhee Kim

Library of Congress Cataloging-in-Publication Data
King, Michael.
    Lorien lost / by Michael King.
        p.   cm.
    "A Wyatt Book for St. Martin's Press."
    ISBN 0-312-14349-4
    1. Time travel—Fiction.   I. Title.
PS3561.I48176L67   1996
813'.54—dc20   95-52745
                        CIP

First Edition: May 1996
10 9 8 7 6 5 4 3 2 1

CONTENTS

CONTENTS

Lorien Lost

THE FIRE

When the town saw the column of smoke rising from Radcliffe House and flocked across the hillside armed with buckets and shovels and axes and jangling lanterns that threw orange ovals of light and long shadows across Milton's unruly lawn, they were much better prepared to save the mansion than they were to save Milton who, marble-white in the bracing night air, merely stared into the flames, still as a statue.

Sooty-faced miners, servants, farm hands, lanky gentlemen in greatcoats that flapped like bats as they ran, all came bumping over the dips and troughs, through the brush and heather, wild-eyed, steel-eyed, charged with fear and excitement and duty. Coaches thundered to a halt. Horses spooked and reared, others neighed, fretting this way and that, never keeping still, no matter how their riders addressed them with the reins. Some men took charge while others followed, some barked orders while others ran, leaped, formed a fire line from the mansion to the well, and a rotating team of swift young boys worked the pump furiously, the bang of it resounding through the clamor like rifle shots.

By the time the firemen ricocheted over the drive in their great brass behemoth and cleared a path through the tumult to string their canvas serpents to the fire, they had all the help they needed. Shovels heaped earth and men heaved buckets full of water and the canvas serpents belched forth jets that rose in clouds of steam, until the only clouds left rose from the patches of derelict flame, and from the glowing ashes slowly turning dormant, and the heavy plumes huffing from panting mouths as they all wound down to catch their breaths.

They looked at one another, perspiring in the cold night, and wondered, now that the fire was out, what to do with Milton.

Most everyone was speechless. A few stared hard at the smoking rafters, and shook their heads in pity. A few turned away and just shook their heads. A few spoke words of condolence to him, tossed tentatively, dubiously, but even these latter kept a critical distance from him, the way they might stand off a ways from an injured bird grounded in their backyard, or a cat, lost and cornered, for fear of startling it.

Milton never moved. He blinked into the last swirls of flames as two boys buried them with quick shovels, and he spoke briefly to someone, distantly, as if he didn't hear his own words, then once again he turned to stone.

He always took two teaspoons of sugar in his Earl Grey. One, two.

The spoon chimed the china as he stirred. Tea-swirl, slowing like a merry-go-round. Nestle the cup in both hands. Warm.

The cup of tea would last him as long as he needed it to last. It always did. Each time he raised the cup to his lips he savored the light breath of steam, and with each soft point of warmth he sipped, he could feel it work its wonders. All the morning business of tie-straightening and shoe-polishing and muffin-buttering finally scattered away and left him to find his natural resting place amid the settling sediment of a featureless afternoon, no alarms, no business, no bothers. It cleaned the slate, and prepared him for his journey.

Finishing his tea, he was ready.

Into the vast vault of perpetual hibernation, past the rows of golden portals, each inviting him. He did not so much as flicker a sideways glance to any of them. He could not afford such a distraction. This was a Larking Day. He could see it. He could feel it. It tingled in his blood, tickled his bones with a lightness born of the very land that awaited him. A cushion of air lightened his step. A giddiness twinkled in his stomach.

Everything had to be just right. The tinkerings had to settle, for one thing, which was not always so easy a task, as these could putter about him for hours. Then there was the entrance itself, which was like the reflection in a pond—the slightest ripple would disturb the image, and leave him stranded. But not today. He could always detect when everything had fallen into place, and on those precious days he took his position amongst it all, and moved within it with a flywheel precision which ratcheted him through a silent walk toward the secret panel, where he had hidden it away for safekeeping.

Careful, careful. Everything just so. The footsteps metered the silence in even measures, past the portraits, past the still-lifes, to the one blank wall. . . .

When he touched a lever concealed inside an ornamental vase, a rosewood panel slid noiselessly aside to reveal a narrow passage. He slipped through as though he were walking between rows of fine china, his step soft, soft.

Down the passage, into the room, the gallery within the gallery.

Soft, soft.

One painting, much taller than himself, in an ornate gold frame. The bottom of the frame nearly touched the floor, the top nearly touched the ceiling. The gold frame was a window opening onto a view of a meadow flecked with rust, wrapped in a blanket of clouds.

Milton closed his eyes a moment, stood very still, collected himself. When he was ready, he opened his eyes again, narrowed them at the gray blanket, searched it patiently.

Lorien? Are you there?

A gust of fog dusted a wall of elms. The elm-tops muttered, fell silent.

He knew that if he stayed very still, he would feel the breeze. The hairs on the back of his neck lifted in anticipation. He did not move. He breathed shallow breaths, drank in the silence, and now the hairs on the backs of his hands prickled.

Lorien?

The cloud layer was an ocean, and he kept searching its depths, half-expecting her to emerge like some translucent ship nodding in the distance, all creaking timbers and snapping sails.

No sails. Not yet.

Was there some faint meadow-scent in the air? Sorrel? Or yarrow?

There—he could see it now: the breeze sent the shallowest ripple through the field of wild oats in the far distance.

Yes: the meadow smells. He drank them in, a spicy wine of peppermint and jasmine and of things he could not name, but recognized. He drank them in long draughts that made his blood tingle.

Smiling, he buttoned his frock coat.

Slowly, he stepped toward the gold frame and held out his hand as though he were about to touch the surface of a vertical pond and didn't want to make waves. Slowly, slowly.

Here I come, Lorien.

His hand was nearly even with the frame, moving very carefully, almost trembling. The grass in the distant field stirred, eddied.

As his hand passed through the frame, it made no ripples. He felt no pond, no surface, only a warm gray wind.

His smile broadened.

He stepped over the frame, and now one foot stood on the smooth wood floor, the other in a patch of brambly mint. He drew his other foot through, and now he was walking in a rambling meadow of wild oats and tangled briars and dockweed that rattled and spilled its dry nettles like rusty pigments of powdered paint as he brushed past them. He rolled a handful in his palm, powdered it even finer, sifted the dust behind him as he picked up his pace. The breeze was stronger now, and tossed a blackbird by like a tumbleweed.

"Lorien! I'm home!"

The cloud cover was one solid layer, a great gray blanket that wrapped the whole countryside snug, and lit it softly with its own diffuse glow. He looked up again, craning his neck and searching all four directions now, cupping his hands to his mouth, calling off to the hills that barely echoed a reply.

The blackbird tumbled up, up, into the gray ocean above.

The wind rippled the hairs on the back of Milton's neck, and teased his cheek.

A giant seedpod blew by, as large as a circus ball.

Lorien called them thistles, but they more closely resembled dandelions—white, fluffy globes with the slightest sheen of blue. The wind plucked them whole from long fluted stems and carried them for miles. Milton would see them all over, many of them wandering aimlessly, but others converging into a stream that cut straight through the middle of the Oat Field. Evidently, there was a single, predominant wind that blew through the valley drawing all the thistles together into a body known as Thistle River. Milton often sat in an oak tree atop a high knoll and watched them gather like wayfaring pilgrims: the air tide would first gently coax them, then tug them, and finally sweep them into the great shimmering exodus that threaded its way through the valley, vast and silent, and finally disappeared in the farthest hills.

The blue-white river had piqued Milton's interest from the moment he'd seen it, and Lorien had obliged him by answering his spate of questions: Thistle River empties into Thistle Bay, where schooners sail in with their cargoes. Some carry barrels of lolligag sand. (It is a dark bronze color, with flecks of midnight-blue and star-yellow. It feels velvety to the touch, and although it's not as potent as sleep sand, a pinch of it will send the most relentless worker into a groggy, wordless daze, fit only for hammocks and hillocks and straw pillows.) Some schooners carry stacks and stacks of burlap sacks filled with fiddler's spice. (The boon of any fiddler: if blended into a tea and drunk at a festive occasion where music is playing, it will compel the imbiber to break out into dance. It is said that different blends will occasion different dances, so that there are waltzing teas and jigging teas and quadrille teas and all sorts of other kinds of teas. The fiddlers choose their blends when they choose their music.) Some carry jars of a special marmalade, veined like orange marble, and so tangy that it will permanently pucker your mouth. (The only way to unpucker yourself is to kiss a dog on the lips. It is so irresistible that many are known to drag their dogs to the table at dessert time so that they may gobble as much marmalade as they like, pecking the dog on the lips with a kiss between each mouthful, until the jar is empty and they are stuffed and round, and the dog is quite cross.) Some ships carried various kinds of tobacco, such as the cherry tobacco which Braymouth used. Had Lorien not told him so, Milton never would have guessed that it was the tobacco, not Braymouth, that made his smoke rings. (This is a characteristic of all Larking Land tobaccos, and each tobacco yields different shapes: Cherry tobacco produces rings. Maple tobacco produces stars. Butter-rum tobacco produces egg-shaped balls that wobble lopsided up into the air, and vanilla blends send smooth disks cascading upward, while menthols send up pyramids. The most startling is a blend called menagerie sweet: give a few puffs, and a parade of smoky animals lopes or gallops or flaps from the bowl of the pipe in great flocks and stampedes. It burns more quickly than the rest, but the spectacle, however brief, is worth it.)

Braymouth, of course, could not be bothered with "critters crawling out of his pipe." He smoked cherry tobacco, and cherry only.

(There is an even more exotic tobacco, which Braymouth simply would not hear of, called tattle-tale tobacco, which works somewhat differently: instead of merely exhaling it, the smoker speaks a few words, and the smoke rises to form letters that spell out whatever he has said. It is quite popular at parties, and often on an afternoon when passing by a festival in full swing, broken phrases can be seen hovering over the rooftops, barely illuminated by the lantern light below, phrases like "Put 'er there, Jed!" and "May I cut in?" and "Save me a piece of that pie." The most intriguing phrases are the ones where the speaker has run out of smoke before the sentence has been completed: ". . . outside in his nightshirt, with a . . ."—". . . seen two geese run as fast as that"—". . . and we never saw him since, the sly old dog." The phrases can linger as long as the next morning, where they will hang, dissipated and stretched by night breezes into an elongated cursive, but still legible to any passerby who cares to eavesdrop with a casual glance.)

Braymouth smoked cherry tobacco, and cherry only.

For all there was of Larking Land to see, Milton never ventured very far. He would spend most of his time looking for Lorien, and once he found her, he would spend most of his time talking with her, and looking through the Book of Days. Sometimes after they had found each other they would explore some nearby copse or glen, but typically, having talked himself blue, Milton would fall asleep on some inviting hillock before they had walked twenty yards. Today he decided to follow Thistle River upstream, to find its source.

Perhaps that's where Lorien is always flying off to, he thought, squinting upstream.

Down through the mint patch, down through the dockweed, down through the bed of bluebells (which really did ring—or rather, jangle—as he trod through), to the blue-white river . . .

The oats and weeds came up to his elbows. He tilted this way and that, balancing his arms like a tightrope walker as he zigzagged through a tangle of cotton grass, then loped down the hill on the other side. The grass had dusted his jacket, leaving a pungent smell.

Down through the switchbacks, down through twitching cattails . . .

He zigged, he zagged, and he tottered somewhat clumsily, until he made his way down the slope to the edge of a wide open plain of oats that looked like a great blond sea. It covered miles, reaching the base of the far mountains to the east, which were patchworked in shades of lavender and forest-green. On one summit, he saw what appeared to be a dim star that had settled there. He narrowed his eyes keenly toward the summit, but it was too far away to discern any detail.

He waded into the field, first ankle-deep, then knee-deep, then hip-deep most of the way as he approached Thistle River, but in places the oats came up to his shoulders, so that parting them became great work, and he eventually decided it would be easier to avoid the deep patches altogether and make his way to the river by a more roundabout path. This is exactly what he did, and had

Lorien been watching from her vantage point, she might have seen a very long and snaky path cut through the Oat Field that afternoon—except, no sooner had he parted the great yellow stalks than they unruffled themselves and resumed their tall stature in his wake, erasing his path.

Down to the blue-white river . . .

The river bowed the tops of the oats so that they laid nearly flat, the way grass does at the bottom of a new stream, giving the thistles a smooth channel through which to flow. As the thistles themselves were far too light to bow such stalks, Milton could only surmise that the wind current was responsible, and his conjecture was confirmed the closer he came: the wind grew stronger and stronger, and began to tug him, like the thistles, toward the swift-flowing stream.

He stopped at the bank. Here the oats rose nearly to his shoulders. The thistles billowed by, falling and rushing over each other, bounding like sheep.

From the east, he heard the steady *clop* of hooves.

Not the four-legged *clop* one normally expects of hooves. Braymouth ran on two legs. He used his other two to pull his hay cart, sedan-chair-style. And when he was not pulling the cart, he needed at least one hoof free to nurse his corncob pipe.

He trotted through the field toward Milton, cutting his own path as he went. He pulled a mountain of hay behind him and huffed peevishly, his donkey ears flat back against his head. He stopped on the opposite bank to rest a moment, and did not see Milton immediately. When he did see him, Braymouth didn't take much notice of him.

"Where's Lorien?" Milton asked.

"Do I ever know?" Braymouth's great donkey lips quivered incredulously at a question he found preposterous. "Hop in!"

He continued to catch his breath until he noticed Milton was still gazing lazily upstream. Braymouth snorted balefully, and stood with his forelegs akimbo, glaring.

"Right!" said Milton, and hopped into the cart.

He sank into a bed of freshly cut oat stalks. The cart jostled and rose. He heard Braymouth grunt and complain, heard the creak of the wheels, and soon they began to trundle eastward. Milton put a stalk of straw between his teeth, laced his fingers behind his head, and watched the sky scroll by. The rhythmic swaying of the cart was like the rocking of a cradle, and the creaking of the wheels was a hypnotic singsong. The bed of oats was so lush and soft and smelled so aromatic that Milton nearly fell asleep, and had to be dumped out of the cart when they had finally reached the hilltop. Milton shook straw from his hair, which had turned into a fright wig.

Braymouth glared. He pulled out his corncob pipe, tamped it full of cherry tobacco, struck a match on his hind horseshoe, lit the bowl.

Puff, puff.

"No sight of her yet," a voice fluted.

Lampyridae.

He floated into view, his feet slowly paddling the air. His paper lantern, which had looked like a star from a distance, was now a dim moon orbiting around him, lit by fireflies. His skin was moon-white, except for his cool blue lips, and his pantaloons were freshly poured moon-cream, whipped and billowed with midnight wind, which was what made him as light as air.

When Lampyridae saw Milton's straw-laced hair, his barks of laughter spun him head over heels.

"Keep your britches on up there," said Braymouth. "You'll miss Lorien."

"Have you seen her at all today?" Milton craned his neck to address the floating Pierrot.

"Nope!" said Lampyridae, who for some reason had begun to revolve.

As he turned, he also buoyed upward to gain a better view. He scouted out, now north, now east, now south, now west, using his hand as an awning, giving his paper lantern a gentle *tap* which sent its orbit upward in a slow, wide ellipse. With each successive *tap* its orbit reached higher, and after a moment of watching this process, Milton guessed its purpose: Lampyridae was sending up a beacon.

Braymouth sent up his own beacons: the smoke rings.

Where did she go on days like this, Milton wondered.

Sometimes she would take hours to find them. Where was she? Off chasing after schooners loaded deep with midnight sands and strange dark spices and marmalades? Sweeping a cloud floor with a whisk broom? Speckling plover eggs? She could be busied with any of a number of things.

The lamp sank down. A slippered toe sent it gently back up.

Was she spooning song-syrup into crickets' mouths, perhaps? Throwing horseshoes with Braymouth's surly cousins? They were poor sports, he remembered, but somehow Milton could never take their tantrums seriously.

The lamp floated up, the lamp floated down.

She might have been dashing up the staircase inside a cyclone or padding through bluebell deeps or unspooling cloud-fabric to warp and weave onto giant looms, or harlequin-cavorting through Maypole Valley, threading the pole-forest as she went with liquid ribbons. Perhaps she was fetching from a distant library the book called "Milton Radcliffe," where his days collected like fine wines.

Lorien, what's taking you so long?

The lamp floated up, the lamp floated down.

His lips began to form another question, then stopped. The glowing Pierrot was so intent on his revolutions that Milton thought it rude to interrupt, so he waited for some break in his routine when he might ask if he saw Lorien yet, or had seen her at all these past few days, or if he expected her soon. But Lampyridae took no break, and his revolutions began to lull him the way a top lulls a small boy who is fascinated with its spinning, and Milton fell very still and silent, all the questions drained out of him.

Braymouth sucked at his pipe with rubbery lips. His ears twitched. He banged the tobacco out using his hoof, then lit up again, the ash swirling like moths on the breeze. When he gave it a few puffs, the pipe bowl began to glow like the fireflies in the lamp.

"I wonder where she went *this* time," the donkey said at length.

"Don't know," said Lampyridae. When he held his arms out, his revolutions slowed.

Braymouth puffed thoughtfully, and every now and then popped out another smoke ring. The rings never dissipated, only floated, up, up, up. . . .

A breeze stirred the treetops in the distance, rattled the brittle dockweeds nearby, eddied at the base of the distant hills.

Puff, puff.

Milton scanned the clouds.

"Wish she'd hurry up." Braymouth's eyes were two shiny lumps of coal.

Lampyridae's revolutions had evolved into an intricate game: he now tapped the lamp by turns with a gloved hand and a slippered foot. At times he resembled a music-box doll turning serenely to some unheard music, except that he turned on several axes, so that Milton could not tell from one minute to the next which end was up. His heels spun over his head, his cloud-patch gloves were turning one way one minute and the other way the next, and his grin was jumbled somewhere in the middle, topsy-turvy. His lamp tilted like a gyroscope, and when it descended its orange light cast through the tall stalks of wild oats, casting long, spindly shadows. Lampyridae's eyes never left his lamp. As the game accelerated, the fireflies in the lamp's core (which were the source of the light) swarmed faster.

All of Larking Land was silent, except for the soft tapping. The lamp strayed higher, its paper shivering in the dusk breeze. The dockweeds rustled. Milton didn't move.

Tap, tap, tap.

"I think I see her," said Lampyridae.

"Is she carrying the book?" asked Milton.

Lampyridae rose a little to improve his view.

"Yes!"

There: Milton saw her too.

If he didn't know it was Lorien, he would have mistaken her for a kite. Her dress, cinnamon- and poppy-dark, snapped lightly in the wind, and she nodded to and fro during her approach, as though she were on a string. As she dipped down out of the higher currents her motion became more fluid. In a flush of excitement Milton took out his pocket handkerchief and flagged to her vigorously, standing on his toes. Lampyridae floated out to meet her.

She hovered just a few yards away, only slightly above Lampyridae, musing. Then she peeled upward, arched back, and shot off again as fast as she could, not a kite this time but a streamlined lark, darting nip and tuck over thickets and briars toward the ocean of wheat.

Lampyridae followed.

Braymouth extinguished his pipe, waved outraged hooves at the sky, and fumbled for his cart.

And Milton ran with all his might.

Over the thickets, over the briar wood, over the patches of heather and mint, over the high knoll and down the other side, toward the ocean of wheat. A flock of wrens took up the chase now, hollering to each other in their own pennywhistle bird-tongue: "There she goes! That way! Keep with her!" Milton sprinted fast and hard. The faster he ran, the easier it became, until he was swept up in his own momentum. By the time he reached the ocean of wheat and parted its golden waves, he was at full tilt, and filled to the brim with Larking Land: the bluebells clanging, the swish of the wheat stalks, the drumming of his feet, the bird-chatter and the whirring of their wings as they bobbed low, the giant thistles turning in their wake, and the fireflies flaring and flashing in a distant butter-moon as Lampyridae pedaled an invisible unicycle that hurled him on a topsy-turvy path at astonishing speed—all to catch an elusive cinnamon-poppy-lark that waltzed merrily among them, but never very close.

Lorien: Don't stop! I'll run forever!

He didn't stop running or even slow his pace until she ended the wild goose game by settling in the middle of the field, laughing.

Milton finally caught her, sat down beside her.

She had brought the book.

The longer he waited between visits, the thicker the book was. This time it was so heavy Lorien could hardly carry it under her arm. Milton gaped at the sight of it. Had it been that long?

She unhooked the clasps, opening it carefully, as though she were peeling away the wrapping paper of a present she had long anticipated. Milton held his breath.

The longer he waited between visits, the more moths.

She had hardly cracked the cover open when they flurried forth in a whirlwind and scattered in all directions. One landed on Lorien's head like a brooch and fanned her with walnut-dark wings. Chameleonlike, her dress turned the same shade, but other than this, she didn't seem to notice the moth's presence.

They sat down, and looked at the book together.

Called the "Book of Days," it contained all the days that Milton had spent away from Larking Land. They had piled up there in a self-assembling scrapbook that cataloged all the special moments in a mélange neatly arranged day by day, so that turning through the pages was like walking through time again, and reliving it. There were a few actual scraps, like a length of emerald-green ribbon from a package he had bought in Piccadilly Circus, or a postage stamp depicting London that had smeared in the rain, so that Big Ben slid down the streaked blue sky so beautifully Milton couldn't bear to spend it, and had kept it instead. And it contained the wrapper of the absolute best chocolate truffle he had ever tasted in his life, bar none, which he had discovered only last week and had savored on his morning walk down Barking Road all the way to Stepney, and long after. (A breath of that sublime confection wafted up even now as he turned the page, and his mouth watered anew.) But mostly, the book contained photographs taken by some mysterious photographer whose identity Milton could never guess. At first he thought it was Lorien, but then, it couldn't be, because she never saw the pictures until Milton arrived and they looked through the book together. So, who took them?

Even more baffling were the photographs themselves. They were not normal photographs by any means. They were dim and milky, as though they were very old and had been bleached by long exposure to the sun, yet they could not have been more than a few days old, or weeks at the most, because Milton never stayed away from Larking Land longer than that. The details were obscured in a haze, as though he were peering through a window pane that was fogged or dusty or scratched, yet he could always recognize the moment.

There it was: his walk down Tillington Road after a rain, the cobblestones glistening slick—and right next to it, there was the day of the rain. He had looked down at his feet just as the first drops dotted the sidewalk, and it was as though an invisible painter had begun to work up a painting, dotting the walk, dotting his shoes, his coat, his hands as he held them out, his tongue as he tasted the air. And next to it, a photograph of Hyde Park dissolving in an ocean of silver threads.

Then he would find the thing that was different, the thing that didn't match.

There would always be something that didn't fit the way he had remembered it. There would always be some small detail, something he had overlooked at the time, which shed a new light on a moment he had mistaken as ordinary.

At first this had baffled Milton, but after enough returns to Larking Land and subsequent pagings through the book he had begun to discern a pattern: the photographs always revealed to him something that he had missed, and it was usually some little piece of Larking Land that had turned up in some unlikely place, that he hadn't seen at the time. For instance, in the picture of him in repose at the quiet pub where he would sometimes nurse a claret in some late hour and reflect on his day, the picture showed him staring absently into the depths of his wine bottle. He remembered the moment of that reverie, and even remembered admiring the way the light glimmered inside the bottle. But what he had *not* seen at the time was the firefly stirring in those depths, glowing like a ruby—or like one of the sentinels inside Lampyridae's paper lamp.

Another photograph showed Milton bundled in his frock coat on a wintry walk down Tillington Road where the rows of stone houses sent up their columns of smoke all down the lane. He remembered the walk, and all the little things he had noticed, like the way the packed snow crunched and squeaked beneath his feet, and how the frost crosshatched the window glass the way a baker might score a pie crust, and the way the previous night's furious winds had blasted the wooden shutters of the houses with a spray of snow dust that still stuck to them like powdered sugar on a cake. He even remembered stopping briefly to admire those peppery curls flowing up from the chimneys. What he did *not* remember was one particular chimney that sent up not curls but a series of smoke rings. The rings never dissipated, only floated up, up, up . . . like the cherry tobacco rings that Braymouth puffed from his corncob pipe.

And, in another picture of himself walking down Tillington Road, he saw, just over his shoulder, a thistle as big as a melon following him, just a little ways behind.

Most remarkable, the Book of Days.

It was the only time Milton really talked, and he talked a stream of words that no dam could hold back. He would point to each picture, and explain everything in great detail. All the things that everyone else would call trivial, or denounce as foolish or, worst of all, that would cause them to stare in blank puzzlement, he uncorked and let flow until he had said all there was to say about the picture. Lorien would turn the page, and he would spout on again, and so on, until they reached the end.

She rarely said anything. She didn't need to. She listened. Sometimes she nodded; sometimes she asked a question about, say, exactly what *kind* of painting the rain worked up on the sidewalk or exactly what did the snow *say* when it squeaked beneath his feet; but she never interrupted his train of thought until it had run its course, though it might take them over hill and crag and through many twists and turns, until Milton himself quite wondered where he had led them.

All his stories flooded out of him, and when he was done, he felt curiously light, like Lampyridae.

A single moth perched on Milton's finger like a ring, working his wings methodically. Milton studied them: deep powdery swirls, with two moon-white spots that looked like eyes, studying him in return.

Lampyridae said: "Ho, *ho*!"

A hay cart bucked and crashed over the hilltop.

"What's so funny?" Braymouth demanded to know. He huffed and heaved long after he set the cart to rest.

Lorien closed the book, and she and Milton walked a lazy, wordless walk through the meadow. Milton would sometimes pause to point out a patch of cotton grass that was particularly wispy, or an oak that was particularly gnarled, or a thistle that sped particularly fast over the brambles, and Lorien would nod acknowledgment and smile knowingly. Still, she hardly ever spoke. It was as though she understood so much (through an empathy that mystified Milton), and her understanding was so unmistakably manifest in the slightest nods and gestures, that she needed no words. Nor, here, did Milton. They each would rather listen to the silver jangle of the bluebells, and the *swish* of their steps through the dry oats and dockweed.

Milton's attention returned to the quicksilver thread known as Thistle River that weaved its way through the plum-dark hills.

"I've always wondered: where does that wind come from?"

"I'll show you," said Lorien. "Let's go."

And Lorien took to the sky.

Milton followed on foot, trotting behind. Lorien took a long lead, flying low when she reached the river, so that when Milton straggled behind to try an experiment, he lost sight of her. But he couldn't resist the experiment. It was something he had always wanted to do.

He stuck his head in Thistle River.

A stampede of fleecy stars rushed over him.

He reeled backward and fell into a cushion of oats, dazzled, and when he blinked up at the sky he realized that he was lying beneath the river, watching it rush above him. He tried counting thistles, but there were too many at once, and they flowed by much too quickly. He gave up on counting and simply watched the river flow, which sent him quickly off to sleep.

CHAPTER 2

THE VIGIL

Lady Mariah, Milton's closest neighbor, had often noted that the idle rich are given to eccentricity. She found plenty of examples in history to support this. There was the Duke of Sutherland, whose passion was to ride fire engines and the locomotives of the Highland Railway, and who spent £250,000 toward that railway's construction, to indulge his hobby. There was Charles Scarisbrick, who commissioned the architect Welby Pugin to construct an exact duplicate of his family's Gothic estate, the great Scarisbrick Hall in Lancashire, where he lived thereafter in seclusion, refusing to speak even to his steward. And there was the Duke of Portland, who always wore three pairs of socks, carried a handkerchief that was three feet square, and built an underground tunnel a mile and a half long between Welbeck Abbey and the town of Worksop so that he might travel clandestinely to his London house, where he idled in his garden—which was surrounded by an eighty-foot-high fence made of iron and ground glass.

There are many others, each following their own crooked paths to their logical extremes, providing sundry entertainments for those such as Lady Mariah, editor of *Toad in a Hole,* the prestigious society journal, and her subjects—the large body of readers who subscribed to that popular publication, who enjoyed reading about spendthrifts and recluses and mad dukes.

But neither she nor any of the other town gossips knew what went on either in Milton's head or, for that matter, in Radcliffe House. The more imaginative among them made plenty of guesses, and the guesses became muddled in the course of gossip to be confused with fact, so that many rumors surrounded Radcliffe House and its somewhat eccentric occupant. One rumor was that Milton's parents had left him behind to take a summer tour of some far corner of Europe, but had never returned, leaving Milton to be raised by a staff of servants who had tucked the tiny orphan away on a high shelf with the fine china and proceeded to run the house themselves, tossing him only enough breadcrumbs to keep him quiet, and dusting him only when the surrounding plates and vases merited dusting, and otherwise ignoring him entirely, so that Milton never learned of the outside world until a pack of lawyers had discovered the house and the servants and the whole ghastly affair, and set things straight.

Another rumor was that insanity ran in the Radcliffe family, and that both of his parents had gone insane and had abandoned him at the ripe young age of five years old, wherein the same business of the servants ensued, to be set straight by the same pack of lawyers.

Still others speculated that Radcliffe House itself had driven his parents insane, and was slowly working on Milton, unraveling him thread by thread.

One of the more fanciful rumors went like this: It was said that within Radcliffe House there was a tremendous trunk which was filled with missing things. All the things in London that anyone thought they had misplaced had actually disappeared—and reappeared inside Radcliffe's Trunk. The whole house, it was said, was populated with furniture that had by some fashion or another vanished—in a shipwreck, or a fire, or by supposed misshipments of merchandise—so that everything in Radcliffe House really belonged somewhere else, but had found its way to this mysterious orphanage of inanimate objects. Milton himself was a missing thing, a sort of loose end wandering through a house of lost trinkets, waiting for his rightful owner to polish him up and take him home.

Fanciful rumors, and very entertaining. But what did anyone really know of him? In the end, the gossips were left to infer what they could through observation (which was, after all, their chief occupation) and as such, merely concluded that he was, well, an odd sort of fellow. They knew, for instance, that he lived alone in a mansion of two dozen rooms, keeping not a single butler, maid, or footman; that of all the clubs in London, which catered to the most eclectic interests, he belonged to not a single one; that he never carried a pocketwatch and, as a result, never knew what time it was, nor seemed to care; that he read neither *The Times,* nor *Punch,* nor *Puck,* nor Lady Mariah's *Toad in a Hole,* nor any other newspaper, magazine, or journal, respectable or otherwise, so he was not abreast of the current state of affairs, either in London or abroad. They knew that he bought artwork like a boy in a sweetshop, producing his checkbook with a magician's flourish and scribbling out payment to the tune of whatever figure the dealer cared to name, without haggling. And they knew that he never strayed beyond the Thames, in fair weather or foul.

On the rare occasions when he engaged anyone in conversation, they noticed that his eye would sometimes wander, as though his attention were distracted by something flitting by, just off in the distance.

Every Tuesday night, if they happened to be in London, they could see him walking through the fog on his way to Madame Tussaud's Waxworks, where he would walk among the frozen tableaux: "The Royal Family" was a favorite of his, and "Sleeping Beauty." He would stop to scrutinize each one, and when he did, he himself would become very still, so that if anyone were to enter the exhibit to see him there, immersed and unblinking, they might easily mistake him for one of Madame Tussaud's creations.

He would always go on a weeknight, after the crowds had dissipated, and if you happened to see him afterward taking his walk on a foggy evening, bundled in his frock coat, he would appear in the halo of the gaslights as some amiable ghost, gliding noiselessly through the mist, nodding a wordless greeting as he passed, only to vanish again in the fog as suddenly as he had appeared.

An odd fellow, indeed.

It was no wonder, then, that after the fire had been extinguished and the men in black coats and stovepipe hats came and made notes in their ledgers with greasy pencils, and blamed the fire on the fluke of a faulty gas lamp, and took care of all the business of it, still no one knew what to say to Milton Radcliffe. Nor were they particularly surprised when he disappeared. The stovepipe hats had snapped their ledgers shut, bowed gravely, and marched off, and no one had seen Milton since. Radcliffe House stood untouched, its charred timbers and blackened stones turned cold, but no less black than on the day they had burned. Crows now perched there occasionally, and every once in a while *cawed* down into the ruins below.

How do you comfort a ghost?

No one knew. So they waited for him to emerge on his own. When they rode by in their coaches, they stared out at the ruined wing, hoping to see some sign of renewal, but instead finding the same fierce mausoleum risen up out of the ground, caging two, three, four dozen oil and canvas phantoms in spoiled colors, fretting amid the ashes and broken gold frames. On days after it had rained, the steam would rise up off the beams, and children would point and cry out that Radcliffe House was burning down again, until their parents would silence their alarms—but not without looking out themselves, and watching the steam rise, and remembering.

Days passed. Weeks passed.

One crow had built a nest in the remains of the west wing.

But still, no one saw Milton. The street lamps of London searched the night fog for him, casting out their gray halos like lighthouse beacons, but did not find him. When no one was looking, the wax statues in Madame Tussaud's clicked their glass eyes this way and that, first at the clock, then toward the door, expecting to catch a glimpse of him. But they did not see him.

Only the crow watching from the charred rooftop of Radcliffe House knew where Milton was. He heard the footsteps every day at the same time, like clockwork, and sometimes at night, too, shuffling mouse-quiet through the soot, echoing up into the darkness.

The crow cocked his head quizzically.

Caw!

Every day. At the same time.

He kept returning to the wing, again and again, as though it all had to be some terrible mistake. Surely, he thought, some *other* room burned, one of the empty ones, and the Larking Gallery still lay hidden safely away, behind the secret panel, if only he could find it. . . .

Every day, and on many sleepless nights, he walked the wing, and ran his fingers over the walls like a blind man, searching for a secret panel that perpetually eluded him.

The search continued for weeks. Every evening after dinner, he took the same walk. Like a bird caught in a scrambled migration, flying toward winter, he touched down, cocked his head at the ruins, bewildered, then, chilled, flew onward, always thinking that some warmer clime named Larking Land lay just around the corner, untouched, simmering its night grasses, waiting for his step to stir its tangles of weeds again, for his nostrils to drink the sweet air like long-steeped tea.

Sometimes, a name would surface on his lips, and they would pantomime a whisper to the charcoal walls.

Lorien? Can you hear me? I'm back.

He would walk deeper into the blackened hall, printing his footsteps in an ash that was like black snow, blanketing an obsidian canyon.

Lorien, can you hear me? Surely, if I can step through to your world, you can step into mine? I can't find the panel. If you could just step outside a moment and knock on the wall, I think I could find you. Could you do that for me, please?

He listened.

Knock on wood, Lorien, please. If you can hear me, just step out a moment and knock on the wall, so I can find you. This whole place is burnt and charred and everything looks alike, and I can't find you and I can't find the panel. I need that night grass and the thistles and the sweet meadow air, and I need to talk to you about some things, so please, if you can hear me, just knock on wood, Lorien, knock on wood.

He kept listening, looking, appealing to the canyon walls.

He would stop and stand very still, and close his eyes. He listened with his whole body, sensing with every hair on his skin the faintest pulse, the slightest shift in air current, the softest settling of eaves and rafters, the smallest stir of ash.

No clocks ticking. No fire crackling. Barely, his own breath, his heart fluttering.

Knock on wood, Lorien, knock on wood.

"Milton Radcliffe stop collecting? Absurd!"

So hooted Lady Mariah upon hearing Gerard's gossip over their elevenses. "It's impossible! I don't believe a word of it," she said, then crept to the edge of her seat to soak in every detail.

"No one has seen him, hide nor hair, for nearly four months now," he answered, nibbling a tea-cake.

"Since the fire," Lady Mariah added.

"I spoke with Randolph and Charles yesterday. They haven't seen him either. He used to call on them every Thursday, like clockwork, and ogle for hours over the Leighton works. But no one's seen him."

"Perhaps he's discovered other galleries," suggested Lady Mariah. "Galleries outside London."

"He never leaves London," said Gerard. "Not so far as I know."

Lady Mariah's mouth began to water.

"He must be busy with repairs," she suggested, still poised on the edge of her chair.

"You'd think so, except no such repairs appear to be under way. He's left the wing untouched. I rode by only yesterday on my way to Chelmsford and no one was about. There isn't even scaffolding in place."

"What do you suppose he's doing in there?" she asked innocently.

Gerard did not look up from his eggs and muffin. "The same thing he's always done, I imagine. We never did see much of him, even before the fire, did we?"

"But surely, arrangements must be made," protested Lady Mariah. "Carpenters must be contacted, and estimates made, and rubbish removed. If your house catches on fire, you can't just ignore it, Gerard! That's positively absurd!" She sketched an exclamation point on the air with her feather boa.

"Mr. Radcliffe has attended to his own affairs for years," said Gerard. "I'm sure he can continue to do so without our help."

Lady Mariah looked out the window in the direction of Radcliffe House, as if she could look over the hills and years, and see the old mansion as it appeared a decade ago, two decades, a century. It appeared the same as it always had, the same as it was to this day—except for the destroyed west wing. The fire had shocked her not merely because it happened without warning (as fires do), but because, in devouring part of Radcliffe House, it had devoured a belief she held so deeply that she had never questioned it: the belief that Radcliffe House would never change. Watching it burn had been like watching Stonehenge crumble. Little wonder, then, that during the fire Milton had emerged like a jackrabbit smoked out of his burrow. She might have felt better had he scampered in all directions over the hills in a panic, but the way he had only stood there, speechless and blinking, gave her a chill that shuddered through her even now.

"It's a pity, isn't it? His growing up alone," she said to the hills.

Gerard said that Milton did just fine.

Far from agreeing with him, the four dozen oil and canvas phantoms of Radcliffe House rose up a chorus that carried on the breeze all the way to Lady Mariah, who heard it softly, softly touching her window pane: It *is* a pity, a pity indeed.

CHAPTER 3

THE WISH

His lips fumbled the words in his sleep: *Come back, come back.*

Every night, the dream was the same: He relived his last night in Larking Land, and his last conversation with Lorien.

Never before had he seen Larking Land at night. The sky had begun to clear, allowing a few crisp stars to peer through the patches of clouds that remained. The clouds moved swiftly enough for Milton to discern their motion, a great armada of cotton galleons in disarray, trimming mile-high sails to catch celestial trade winds and breeze them off to unknown destinations. The moon, that great pearl of night, cast its light through the tossed armada and gilded the edges of its sails, and found its way through to touch a few hill crests in places, spotlighting an oak tree here, a bramble there, in luminous gray. But the moon itself remained cloaked, and hid from view.

Lorien had concealed something in her hands. "Close your eyes," she said.

He did.

"Open."

A Mason jar, filled with smooth, green-yellow globes.

"Do you know what they are?" she asked. "Pickled wish-plums!" She smiled, as if it were some kind of joke. But it wasn't.

They sparkled just slightly, like the lemon drops he'd sometimes buy at the sweetshop on Oxford Street. When she unscrewed the lid he stuck his nose in and smelled the pickling solution: a tart lemonade.

"The season's over, but I like to keep some all year around. Here." She plucked one out and held it up as though a gem cutter, examining her handiwork, then gave it to Milton. "Eat it, then make a wish. Don't chew. Suck on it slowly. Savor it."

"Do the wishes always come true?" Milton asked, turning the glistening globe in the moonlight.

"If I pickled them right." She popped one into her mouth demonstratively, rolling it on her tongue.

"Hey, look! Your mouth is glowing!"

It was true. Like Lampyridae's lamp, a buttery light shone through her cheeks, colored by her own complexion with a hint of dusty rose.

Milton tasted the wish-plum Lorien handed to him. Its sourness surprised him. He sloshed the ball from one cheek to the other. "Let's see, what should I wish for?"

"Oh, don't wish out loud!" Lorien admonished.

He puckered and smacked his lips, but he couldn't decide what to wish for. He always had trouble deciding on those kinds of things.

He sucked and savored some more.

"Do I have to make my wish now?" he asked.

"No, but don't wait too long," said Lorien.

He waited. He dawdled. He watched Lampyridae pedaling away on the air, sloping up and down invisible hills. Here the moon was so bright it washed out the halo of his paper lantern, so that it hardly seemed to glow any more than, say, the open faces of the daisies, or the white, powdery stems of the lavenders which dotted the hills. But when Lampyridae slipped through the shadow under a tremendous oak bough, his true nature was defined: as he passed through that night within the night, he blazed the deepest blue, and the fireflies, stirring in their swaying lamp, were yellow stars jumbled in a paper moon.

Milton's cheeks felt warm now, and the tartness turned to sweetness. He had strayed into the yarrows up the hill a little way, hands in pockets, rolling what was now a tasty nugget around in his mouth and stopping here and there where a glistening spiderweb quilt or a jack game of acorns played out under a beech caught his eye. He strayed for some time, and by the time the nugget melted to a smooth liquid, he still hadn't thought of anything to wish for, and he had no idea where he was. Then he noticed that the air didn't smell quite right. There was a sharpness to it.

A little band of leaves capered across his path on a distant hillock, muttering in their brittle tongue.

He had turned to speak to Braymouth, but he too was gone. The last line of smoke rings trailed upward like stray circus balloons, growing wider and thinner but never actually dissipating, until they blended into the field of gray, lost to vision, only a trace of cherry tobacco left lingering in the air.

"Braymouth!" shouted Milton.

His voice sounded small.

There was no answer. The wind picked up, stirring complaints from the oak boughs. It rippled the distant field of dusky oats, so they appeared as the surface of a restless sea.

The sea before a storm.

The sharpness in the air tickled his nostrils.

Smoke?

Then he'd seen the fire leaping on the distant hill. He bounded and stumbled over uncertain knobs and dips in the slope, but by the time he reached the fire, it was too late. It had already started to happen:

The midnight sky was melting. It smeared down in deep blue streaks, ran into the trees and knolls, and they all ran together into muddy rivulets that dripped onto the gallery floor. Blackness poured over canvasses like stains, golden frames baked, barked, split, cracked. Oily thunderheads billowed forth from each frame, filling the ceiling, then the top third of the chamber, then the top two thirds, until Milton himself began to blacken with soot and perspire like an overbaked roast of mutton. He shouted into the flames, but his voice was drowned out by the roaring of the fire, which soon licked his boots, his frock coat, his earlobes—

He woke with a start.

He wrapped himself cocoon-tight in his blankets, and waited for his hard breathing to subside.

Only then, after his pulse had slowed back to its gentle hourglass ticking and his feet had stopped twitching beneath the sheets and the last residue of the recurring nightmare had washed out on the night tide to give way to still, stark sunrise, did he proceed to make the wish.

"Lorien, I wish that you'd come back."

Dust motes spiraled listlessly through the first bar of daylight, feathery gondolas foundering slowly down, slowly down.

"I wish that Lorien would come back."

By imperceptible degrees, morning deepened, brightened. A single, sunny square lit the floor. Somewhere outside, a wren piped up.

"I wish that Lorien would come back."

The wren continued, hesitantly.

The room warmed.

Milton emerged from his cocoon, dressed, shuffled off to the kitchen to prepare his morning tea.

Two teaspoons of sugar. One, two.

And all through his breakfast, every rattle of his cup, every sloshing in the teapot, every brittle chattering of china spoke the same words: *Don't wait too long. . . .*

The walks and wishings went on like that for weeks that stretched into months, during which no one saw Milton Radcliffe, and Milton himself saw nothing beyond the walls of Radcliffe House, which seemed to grow smaller and smaller with every passing day. He could not understand how the house that had been a whole world to him suddenly felt so close and, in some strange way, inhospitable, as though the very walls begged him for his own sake to leave. But he could not shake these impressions; he huffed now on his walks like a locomotive, his face set like cast iron.

He began looking.

He looked everywhere.

He looked in galleries, in private studios, in private collections. He haunted every auction and estate sale in London. He swept his bull's-eye lamp through every dark corner where he suspected he might, just might, find his lost treasure sunken away: his portal, his lost gate to Larking Land. No crevice escaped illumination. No corner of any pawnshop was too cluttered or too musty or too junk-filled and forsaken to escape Milton's rummaging. He dug like a rabbit in a burrow, leaving not a single rug, snuff box, or chest of drawers unturned.

A window, please? Just one?

Pissarro? No thank you. Sir Edward Burne-Jones? Yes, it's beautiful, thank you very much, but no. No, no, it's not the price, that has nothing to do with it. Don't you see?

I need to go to Larking Land.

But his search was fruitless. Most of the places turned up nothing at all, only a few had any original artworks of note, and of them, only a very few turned up anything by the mysterious Jonathan Larking, none of which were for sale. Milton tested this very severely, but no sum that he could bring to bear upon them, however great, could persuade the owners to part with their rare masterpieces, so that in the end Milton could only walk away defeated, and empty-handed.

In this way, Milton resembled a sailor stranded in a foreign port trying to bargain his way aboard a ship that was headed for his home. What's worse, the natives didn't speak his language. When he told them that he didn't have any particular Larking painting in mind, but that he simply must have *a* Larking painting, any Larking painting, they responded by asking if they might instead interest him in this very fine piece by Turner. Well, how could Milton possibly explain?

CHAPTER 4

THE PAVILION JOURNAL

There was one point upon which Mr. Samuel Wellington, bookseller and sole proprietor of Wellington's Antiquarian Books, was very clear. That point was this: He had no interest in books. To Samuel Wellington, the book-selling trade was a business, and he a businessman, and that was the whole of it. He bought, he sold, he bartered, he made bids, and he made a healthy profit (sometimes). Through his skill and thrift and good hard business sense, he kept the small but respectable ship named Wellington's Antiquarian Books afloat on the sea of commerce, and of this he was fairly proud.

He had come to Radcliffe House on business. His business being books and not paintings, he felt somewhat out of his element on this particular errand. Yet he was convinced that he had an item that Mr. Radcliffe could not refuse.

Mr. Wellington stood in the foyer before a tall mirror whose glass was all scratched and fogged.

"I'll be with you in one moment," a voice came from one of the rooms. He could not tell from which.

Odd, he thought, that one so well off has no footman or butler. But then, he had heard that Mr. Radcliffe was an eccentric. The bookseller had seen the idle rich before, so he didn't think much of it. Still, the place was uncommonly dusty.

He consulted his watch. He was on time. In fact, it was several minutes past their appointment.

He studied the carved wooden frame of the mirror, and found at the top a small face looking out

amid carved vines and leaves that twisted down around the glass. The face regarded him. He regarded the face. They regarded each other for some time, until Mr. Wellington consulted his watch again, then began peering experimentally into a large empty vase.

Cobwebs. A spider?

He cleared his throat conspicuously.

Finding that no help, his eye began to roam into the surrounding gloom. The foyer led to a large, sullen room. Experimentally, he poked his head in.

A faint but unmistakable odor of mildew permeated the room, the same smell that steeped old trunks and neglected attics. Thick, solemn curtains forbade nearly all light, so that it took a minute or two for Sam Wellington's eyes to adjust to its dimness enough to perceive what lay within. There was little to see, but what little he saw struck him as a bit curious: Nothing had been polished in months, or longer, so that everything had a dull, lackluster appearance. Not a single painting decorated the walls (decidedly odd for an art collector), nor did any statuette or figurine adorn the room. The display cabinet was empty. The mantel, bare.

He found a single candlestick on a sideboard whose brass knobs were encrusted with patina. The candlestick offered no candle. Its brass stem was speckled with green flecks, like the liver-spots on an aged hand.

In the corner of the far wall, the wallpaper had begun to peel and flake.

It was as though the place had never been lived in. Either the tenants had moved out years ago, or else they had never quite moved in. Sam Wellington, examining the surrounding gloom, could not quite tell which.

As his eye scanned across the floor, he discovered it had lost its varnish long ago, and was pocked haphazardly with the scuff and heel marks of boots. Upon closer examination (and a little experimental poking into adjacent rooms), Sam Wellington noted that the train of shoeprints ran in regular paths from one room to another within the manor's interior. But none of them entered the foyer. In fact, the foyer floor was untouched. Though Sam Wellington was not normally given to fancies, he could not help but imagine what kind of arrangement would produce such an effect: a train of fish-pale manor dwellers shuffling down their tracks. He could see their saucer-eyes darting in the darkness, hear the rhythmic scuff of their cracked-leather boots scraping at the floor of their dank grotto, shaving it away.

He cleared his throat again.

He was relieved to find that his host, though a trifle pale, was not exactly as he had imagined.

"Milton Radcliffe," Milton introduced himself, offering his hand.

"Sam Wellington, bookseller." The two shook hands firmly and got down to business.

Mr. Wellington explained that he was not an art collector, but rather, that he was in the business of selling books of a great variety and value. In the course of his rummaging he had discovered the journal of the famous painter and sculptor Jonathan Larking. He had seen Mr. Radcliffe's advertisement in *The Times* offering a handsome sum for any painting by Larking, and while he had no painting to offer, perhaps he could interest Mr. Radcliffe in the journal.

At the mention of Larking's name, Milton had become rapt in attention, and before the bookseller could shift into his lecture defending the journal's authenticity, Milton asked him to name a price and scribbled out a check without ado—without even inspecting the journal, in fact.

The eccentric rich, thought Sam Wellington. Spendthrifts all.

As he left, however, he began to debate whether or not he had made a careless mistake. Mr. Radcliffe had not written his check with the air of boredom so common to wealthy collectors. To the contrary, he'd worked up to a fevered pitch. Reflecting at length, Mr. Wellington began to think he had indeed made a grievous error in naming his sum, and spent the better part of his trip home browbeating himself for his miscalculation. How could he have been so careless? The only explanation he could find was that he had been somewhat distracted by the strange surroundings, and especially the sight of the ashen-men shunting about in the abandoned room. He took a long walk that afternoon in the sunshine, and following dinner and a very fine cigar, he'd managed to rid himself of that disturbing notion altogether.

Blank spine. Blank cover. No title. Sun-bleached edges of pages. Open it up: the smell of decayed poppies and aged leather.

Milton turned to the cover page, and found penned in flamboyant, fluid strokes:

Pavilion Journal. Volume One. Summer, 1851.

He recognized the handwriting even before he read the signature at the bottom of the page, a cursive he had seen hundreds of times before, on every portal he had ever stepped through. He saw the lively, whimsical letters frolicking in his mind:

J-o-n-a-t-h-a-n   L-a-r-k-i-n-g

He turned the page. The following journal entry was written in the same fluid hand:

20 June

Our secret hideaway has been discovered.

When Lorien and I unpacked our coach, we found a stowaway in our wicker basket, which had originally been solidly filled with linens. The stowaway? Little Heather, of course. Who else could perform such an antic?

Still, we were shocked. But I supposed we were not half as shocked as her mother will be when her daughter doesn't come home for supper. She'll throw an elegant fit, I'm sure, as is the prerogative of any mother who has been frightened with the disappearance of her child, though I do imagine that Isadora is more accustomed to such shocks than most parents, Heather being the adventurous imp that she is.

I tried to scold her, but it was of no use. The sight of her popping out of the basket in a flurry of cloth was just too precious. What can we do? We've decided to let her stay. I will slip into Barnstaple tomorrow and send a letter to Isadora letting her know that her daughter is safe with us, but I simply don't have the heart to send her back. Incorrigible though she is, she is also a dear. Tut-tut, little Heather.

I enjoy watching her. She wanders off into the wild oats singing to herself (a little echo of her mother), and she is quite entertaining. She bumbles from one bramble-patch to the next, fruitlessly chasing after butterflies or sticking her nose into patches of wild mint. She often plays a game of some sort where she bears a long reed as a scepter and marches off into the bluebells, talking to herself. She is so tiny, and the bluebells here are so extraordinarily tall and lush that she disappears in their midst. I can hear her disembodied voice rise up from them, but I cannot make out the words. (How I wish I could!) She plays in there for hours, until we call her in for supper.

Sometimes she digs in the earth, hunting for insects. She comes back with her dress dirty, her face dirty, her hair dirty, her shoes dirty, and of course she drags the dirt all through the pavilion without any notion of what she's done. It's quite marvelous.

We are shy a few linens, I suppose, but definitely much richer for having our little guest.

Milton wet his lips, turned the page, kept reading.

2 July

I sketched Lorien all afternoon today. She fell asleep in a bed of thyme on a hillock, and I crept up on her and sketched her face a dozen times or more. I found myself asking the question: How many times can I sketch this face and still find something new? We've been married for ten years, and the discoveries continue. It is an interesting puzzle, these expressions within expressions, like those Russian dolls that are hollow inside: you open one up, and find another, and another, and so forth. A most curious business. But then, Lorien is that way, come to think of it. Dolls within dolls.

9 July

Today little Heather returned to her voice lessons all on her own. She was singing her nonsensical singsongs the way she always does when, out of the blue, solfeggio *syllables began creeping in. I don't know whether she was using them correctly, but I recognized them from hearing Isadora in her own practice. They were* solfeggio, *bubbling out of Heather like soda bubbles. Soon she was singing scales. Not in any disciplined way, but with some regularity, and very tunefully.*

She is clearly a Feur-De-Lys. Song runs in her blood. I daresay she may follow in her mother's footsteps yet, and become opera's next great lyric soprano. Who can tell?

1st July

I've enough sketches now that I am ready to start working on the stone. There is a whole summer within that stone, and somewhere in that summer walks another lady, waiting for me to let her out. I simply must find her.

I know now that this secret retreat was the best idea I've had for nourishing my heart. Only in this solitude and quiet can I catch the faintest glimpse of that lady in the stone. She becomes clearer every day, and I've no doubt that freeing her will be my greatest work yet.

Milton's hand trembled now as he jumped a few pages further to skim a later entry, then another and another, until he found the moment, the one telling moment that he hoped he would find:

18 August

[Here the script was long, tilted, ecstatic]
My, my, my.

I have chased after her for over two months. In the last five days I have hardly set down my chisel except to eat the snacks that little Heather brings me. I had lost count of the days completely. I was in hot pursuit, and could not afford to stop for fear of losing sight of her. But last night my efforts came to fruition: I finally found the woman in the summer within the summer. I have found her, and I have released her.

She amazes me.

I finished her in the early evening, just as the crickets were starting up. But I stayed up all night without sleeping a wink. How could I? I only wanted to walk around her in endless circles and see her standing there in a halo of white powder, this elusive woman who finally allowed me to bring her here to this special place. I cannot describe how gratifying the sight of her was, no longer shimmering beneath the surface of a stone sea, but standing before me, fresh and alive.

I have decided to keep her here in the pavilion, forever. I will not take her back to the city. She belongs here, in this place. I cannot explain this decision, and am very glad to know that I will not have to, because no one will know of her except Lorien and me (and of course, little Heather, but our secret is safe with her). No one will know, so no one will ask for explanations.

Like this place, she will be our hidden treasure, to enjoy when we return next year, and every summer thereafter.

Milton read the entry again. He read further, and walked with Jonathan Larking through a meadow somewhere in Devon. He could almost smell the yarrow-wine again, and see the great muscled beeches reaching two dozen knobbed fingers up to clutch at the gray blanket above where, somewhere, Lorien chased a tumbleweed blackbird. He could almost see the confetti of moths scattering in all directions, and feel the rushing of Thistle River blowing through him, washing everything away, rinsing the hills.

Take me back.

The page shivered in his hand. Off in the west wing, a rafter groaned, sifting ash down in a fine dust like snow.

Lorien, listen: I've lost the window, and now I'm trapped here, and I cannot find any other way to get back, so just wait for me in Devon, wait for me in Devon, and I'll come and meet you as soon as I can, I promise.

He didn't know why she had returned to such a faraway place, but did it matter? She had returned. The pickled wish-plum had worked. His wish had come true.

His hands twitched over the pages, his eyes raced. Devon? The hills of Devon? Where was that? Milton had never left London, ever. His hands turned frosty.

Lorien, please wait. I don't know what happened. I wished for you to come back, but I don't know where Devon is, but I'll find it, I promise. Just wait for me, please?

The frost crept through him, the way it crystallizes on a window pane, imperceptibly, one crystal at a time. He tried to keep reading, but the ice spread through his body, paralyzing him, and a shiver ran through his bones.

It had rained the night before in the west wing, and the rafters steamed. Atop them, a single crow fanned invisible flames with shiny wings and, peering sharply down into the mausoleum below at the phantoms of canvas and oil milling among the waste, cried his alarms.

Please wait.

CHAPTER 5

THE EXPEDITION ANNOUNCED

"Milton Radcliffe lead an expedition? Absurd!"

Lady Mariah's feather boa was all in a tizzy now.

Gerard smoothed the page of *The Times* upon the table before her, so she might read it with her own eyes. She looked down, appalled.

AN AMAZING DISCOVERY!

The works of the renowned painter and sculptor Jonathan Larking have been sought after by collectors for years. Until recently, scholars had believed all his pieces to be either on display in private galleries or destroyed. However, the discovery of Mr. Larking's private journal has revealed the existence of a secret cottage wherein the painter retreated for the summer months to create what he considered his greatest works. According to the journal, his masterpiece, a life-size statue of his wife Lorien, was created there as a permanent installment, and is believed to remain there to this day. Mr. Milton Radcliffe, art collector and owner of the journal, will launch an expedition to recover the statue, and is presently seeking qualified persons to accompany him.

It went on to describe the requisites for applicants and provide an address where inquiries were to be sent, but Lady Mariah could read no further. Gerard frowned at the advertisement awhile before reclaiming his paper, and promptly hiding behind it.

"He's as reclusive as a dormouse," Lady Mariah continued. "He's practically an invalid, especially since the fire. He's not fit to cross the street without holding someone's hand, and anyone who would follow him on an expedition would have to be twice as crazy as he is!" She guzzled her tea for emphasis.

"Men can be hired for any job if the price is high enough," Gerard guffawed from behind his paper. She looked offended. Pouting primly, she refilled her teacup.

"He'll turn back after a few days, I suspect. Or else he'll get lost in the hills, or held up by some highwayman, and we'll never see him again."

"We never see him now," countered Gerard.

"I read in *Plimton's Gazette* just the other day that Isambard Smyte held up another coach, right down on Rochester Way not a day's ride from here." Lady Mariah looked out the window as though she could see the infamous highwayman and his henchmen thundering up the road toward their home, and for a moment she fell silent.

Gerard peered briefly over his newspaper with an air of concern, then disappeared behind it again, muttering something about how Mr. Radcliffe could take care of himself. In return Lady Mariah only arched an eyebrow in indignation, then went back to busying herself with her meal, and when that was done, with anything else that might keep her occupied until she could learn more.

The news of the lost Larking statue sparked great interest in the artistic community, and even attracted a competitor, a well-known aristocrat by the name of Adrian Plackett, who claimed to have the most impressive private art collection in all London. He was fond of proving his point by giving tours through the private museum within his mansion, wherein he pointed to various canvases along the way with an ebony cane as a gamesman might point to the taxidermic trophies of his hunts.

The collection consumed nearly all of his time, not simply because it was growing steadily larger (though that was certainly the case), but because every piece in the collection was in a constant state of secret rebellion against him. The paintings refused to stay straight on the wall, but always inched a trifle clockwise here or a hairsbreadth counter-clockwise there, so that they required repeated realignment. The brass candlesticks refused to retain a shine and scratched altogether too easily, so that some servant was either polishing or buffing out the scratches, one or the other, at all times. The pieces of fine china rattled when anyone walked by, suggesting they were not properly seated in their display, and so required constant rotating and resettling into their places, after which they still rattled.

The most unruly of the rebels was the mob of statuettes, which conspired against him by altering their poses in subtle ways so as to ruin the harmony of the Diorama in which he had meticulously arranged them. Cicero would shunt his elbow intrusively into the Grecian athlete, and of course Adrian couldn't have that. Napoleon would shift his eyes to look in a scandalous way at the young water-nymph, and Adrian certainly couldn't have that. The Etruscan warrior's spear threatened to poke delicate Cupid. Theseus stepped on a dancer's foot. Marcus Aurelius jostled a rearing horse. There was just no end to it.

Every few months Adrian would employ the tactic of "divide and conquer" and disperse the statuettes on various mantels and display shelves throughout the gallery, but the strategy always misfired: if they looked awkward and inharmonious on the display table, they looked far more awkward and inharmonious scattered through a dozen rooms. Aristotle's eye would wander to some other place it shouldn't, and King George's sword would poke something else, and so forth. So Adrian would regroup them and resort to his former ploy of confounding his antagonists by shuffling them ruthlessly in innumerable arrangements and rearrangements within their Diorama.

Thus Adrian Plackett waged his war of attrition, forever putting down skirmishes.

He knew the source of the problem: His collection lacked leadership. They were a people without a ruler. He needed to find a single work of art so elegant and imposing that the power of its presence would dominate the rest. He realized that all the best collections had this. "The Crown Jewel of the Collection," it was always called. It provided focus. It provided order. As soon as he found *his* Crown Jewel, all the other pieces would fall into place. The skewed paintings would snap to their perpendicular position in rigid attention. The brass would remain smartly polished. The china would cease its discontented rabble, and even the mob of statuettes would agree to terms and finally fall in line. And wouldn't that be a load off Adrian's mind? Perhaps then he could get a good night's sleep. Order would be restored.

With this goal in mind, he scoured galleries all over London. He attended auctions. He approached famous painters to inspect their studios in search of royal blood, sure that he would recognize it by some awe-inspiring glimmer that would penetrate him to his very bones—but he never found it. He searched for years without success, firing great volleys of checks in all directions, and bringing home whole legions of artworks, from ruby-studded jewelry to life-size sculptures to paintings as tall as the vaulted ceiling of the Plackett Gallery. After a while, he began to suspect that he was going about the whole thing wrong. Perhaps he was looking in the wrong places. Surely something worthy of the title "Crown Jewel of the Collection" would not give itself up easily.

Where might he find it?

Locked in some high tower with a dozen ancient heirlooms, perhaps? Or barricaded in a nobleman's castle keep?

Or exiled in some secret summer cottage, waiting to be discovered?

When he had seen the handbill announcing the expedition, Adrian's palms itched, and his fingers instinctively fell to his pen and checkbook.

AN AMAZING DISCOVERY!

His face flushed, and immediately he set the machinery of his mind to drawing up great charts and schemes and diagrams.

"I must talk to this Mr. Radcliffe," he said to himself. For an instant, he saw an image of the statue looking back at him: an elegant arch of the eyebrow, a regal carriage of the chin.

"Yes. Mr. Radcliffe and I must have a little talk."

CHAPTER 6

NIGHT VISITOR

The ghost stirred, warmed, breathed.

And the spectral figure that was Milton Radcliffe heated into animation, coursed blood, flinted a spark in his eyes, which now gleamed as they swept hungrily across each page of the book that had resuscitated him. He combed every entry for clues, planning and plotting, a fervor flushing his cheeks, a smile of hope curling his lips.

He made his plans and, by day, walked among the living.

At night, thoughts ran like mice around and around in his head.

The *Cosmographie.* He had opened the *Cosmographie.* How could he have been so foolish?

Perhaps it had smelled the dust rising from those pages as he took down the atlas for the first time in years to look for Devon. A fever had shuddered through his frame as he had touched the spine of the old relic. It had so overwhelmed him that he had nearly snapped the volume shut and tossed it into the fireplace, but it was the only book in the library that contained any maps, so he was stuck.

Had it smelled the tome-dust? Was that how it knew? Was that why it had returned?

Or had it simply read his mind? Thulemander had warned him that it might have special powers. The thought-mice gnawed and nibbled and turned circles in mad tail chases through the night. And his bed became cold as a grave.

A sound returned to him that he had half forgotten, growing steadily louder, and closer now than it had come in years. As soon as he heard the vast flapping of wings reflect off the hills like muffled rifle shots, heard them home in toward Radcliffe House, toward his very room to fan the beeches not twenty yards from his window, so that the trees lolled their heads this way and that like drunken giants, a coldness poured through his veins like liquid lead, and he pulled the sheets tighter around him.

It's back.

The beeches were staggering now, raving. A maelstrom of wingbeats cracked the air directly above Milton's room, and the roof creaked and groaned under some tremendous, lumbering weight.

Go away.

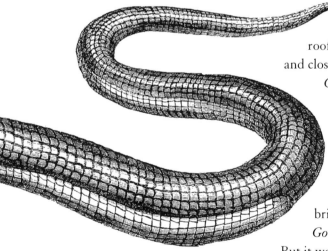

The pressure on the roof shifted. The rafters groaned. Something clenched the roofbeam. Milton clutched two fistfuls of bed sheets and closed his eyes.

Go away. I'm not turning back this time. I'm not turning back. You've cheated me out of too much. I have to go this time, because Lorien is waiting for me. I'm going, I am really going, so just leave me alone and let me go. Stay away from me.

An exhalation now, long and mean, like a ruptured bellows. Then, the smell of soot and brimstone.

Go away. Please. Go away!

But it would not go. All night long, the telltale rasp of scales on shingles, a taste of sulfur in the air, and a splintery creak of gripped roofbeam betrayed the night visitor's presence. Panic swam in Milton's mind for hour upon hour, fermenting into fever. He finally fell asleep in a delirium, the intruder circling through his dreams, fanning them into nightmares with leathery wings, nightmares that would not cool.

In the morning, the break of day evaporated the stain of the previous night's incident as though it were a bad dream, and Milton carried on with his preparations. But every night, the visitor returned.

CHAPTER 7

PUZZLE PIECES

Philippe twirled his mustache thoughtfully as he watched the Diva's performance from the wings. When her performance ended, he peered through a pair of opera glasses to study the faces of the audience, and discovered the usual: the empty chairs told him how many were offended deeply enough to walk out. Those who were merely shocked remained in a chilly silence. The baffled applauded politely, with blank expressions. And the rest—always the majority—thundered applause, shouted such accolades as "Bravo!" and "Encore!" and threw roses.

He turned his gaze on the Diva as she scooped up a bouquet with a gracious curtsy.

She fooled them, he thought. She fooled them again.

As he watched her expressions and the easy way she blew kisses to the audience, he realized how much of the Diva he saw that her fans missed. He had seen her too many times, watched too many rehearsals to be easily taken in. When she made her exit into the wings, he smiled weakly, and she smiled confidently back as she passed, but she retreated to her dressing room for much longer than usual. It was not until they relaxed in the parlor of the hotel the next night that they spoke.

"They adored you, of course," said Philippe as he lit a cigarette. "Most of them."

"Of course," she agreed, sipping her wine.

"But you are dissatisfied with your performance," he said.

The Diva nodded.

Thinking that she might elaborate, Philippe waited a moment, puffing languidly, but the Diva had become interested in some distant point in the room, and said nothing more.

"You never used to forget the words to '*Tourte de la Fou,*'" remarked Philippe.

"They didn't notice."

"Because most of them don't speak French."

They both fell silent, Philippe casting a glance her way every now and then. If she returned his glance at all, it told him little. If she ignored him, he would study her, looking for signs. During dinner, her appetite had been that of a bird. A bad sign, thought Philippe. She finished her wine a little too quickly, looking thoughtfully out the window at the smoky yellow street. "I need a holiday," she said to the window pane.

Philippe mulled that over before he answered.

"Your last engagement is only a few days away. After that, Paris?"

She frowned dubiously, her eye escaping down some distant view, and from that frown Philippe knew she was testing the waters, finding some warmer than others, still undecided where to dip in. Where will she find the cure for what ails her? In the mountain range of pastries in the window of the boulangerie? In the sundial of shadows that fracture through the park benches at the Place de Vosges to cast their hours upon the ground?

There was a crumbled little café on the rue de Tournelles where she dragged him every night when they were last in Paris, and where they had dined elegantly among peeling shutters and flaking paint and smooth worn wooden tables that leaned like the Tower of Pisa among wine-stained grinning old men who had just come in from making things with their hands or talking to old vines. Might she find her cure in there, hidden among the spoils and ruins of half-eaten meals?

In Paris, there was a narrow street that was always filled with pigeons. She had insisted on riding the tallest bicycle she could find for no other purpose than to send the pigeons up in squalls all about her, as a sort of game. Might she find it there, among their flock?

Later that night, she took a walk, alone. Another bad sign. She knew how it worried him for her to walk alone at night. (Had she already forgotten the incident with that pickpocket in York, just four days ago? Would she ever think twice before strolling down another strange city street at night?) All Philippe's lectures and pleadings in defense of caution had won him just this small concession: she now only walked when she needed to walk, which meant she only walked when she had become surrounded with puzzle pieces that had become too scattered and jumbled to ignore, and that needed sorting out.

Of course she forgot the words, thought Philippe ruefully.

He gathered her things in her hotel room, making last-minute preparations so they would not miss the morning coach. While so doing, he let his eye roam across her desk, and couldn't help but notice an advertisement she had clipped from *The Times*. He examined it casually.

AN AMAZING DISCOVERY!

He read it once, drummed his fingers on the desktop while he read it a second time, then leaned back in the chair and lit a cigarette while he considered the message. Now it was Philippe who was surrounded with puzzles. What did it mean? Was this what had upset her? He remembered, vaguely, that her mother had been friends with an eccentric painter. . . .

It was a two-cigarette problem, at least. By then, she would have returned. Perhaps by then she would be ready to discuss it. If not, he would return to studying her expressions and guessing how he could best placate her while still keeping to their schedule. It was his ability to read her moods while simultaneously fending off innkeepers, impresarios, and impatient coachmen that made him the first-rate personal manager that he was.

He waited. He smoked. He watched the curls of smoke weave themselves into pictures of singers and theatres and crazy painters until he dozed in their midst, a little worried but by no means alarmed by the singer's long absence. He took some comfort in knowing that, even if he had tried, he could not possibly have talked her out of her night walk. He took more comfort from the fact that her mysterious migrations never took her too far afield. She always returned, sometimes hours, sometimes days later, but she never missed a coach, never missed a rehearsal, never missed a performance. Not yet, anyway.

She will return soon enough, he thought, and finally surrendered to sleep.

An eccentric painter splashed wild things in great sweeping brush strokes all through his dreams. . . .

CHAPTER 8

A MAN WHO DID NOT ASK QUESTIONS

Milton began the interviews.

The interviews always went the same way: He asked the interviewee his list of questions, then the interviewee asked his own questions of Milton. The applicants answered Milton's questions readily and easily (though sometimes with a look of puzzlement, as though they did not understand why he would ask such a question). Milton answered theirs with considerable difficulty. They made all sorts of inquiries for which he was not at all prepared. How did he know the journal was authentic? What led him to believe the statue was still intact? What method did he use to deduce the pavilion's exact location? What kind of evidence did the journal provide upon which to make such deductions? Exactly what kind of structure was this pavilion? What dangers did the intervening terrain impose, and how did Milton plan to overcome them? And a great many other things, none of which had really occurred to Milton. He floundered through them, taking copious notes as he went, but invariably he would fail the test. Each applicant would announce that he was not interested, bow gravely, and promptly exit, leaving a bewildered Milton to enlarge his list of questions, and scratch off another name from his roster of potential expeditioners.

Thus the one list grew longer while the other grew shorter, until he met an interviewee who did not ask questions.

Mr. Crum.

Short. Sallow. Plainly dressed. A light black stubble that did not qualify as a beard. Greasy hair that stuck out in tufts on either side of his head beneath his hat. A perpetual grin.

His handshake was wiry, limber. As Milton showed him to the den, his eyes wandered over the sparse decorations of Radcliffe House. Keen eyes.

Milton asked his list of questions. Mr. Crum dispatched them neatly. When it was his turn to question his host, Mr. Crum only grinned agreeably, hands folded in his lap.

Milton was a schoolboy let out early. No exams! Hurrah!

He hired Mr. Crum on the spot.

They shook hands. They set a date. Mr. Crum volunteered to make the preliminary preparations. Meanwhile Milton, greatly relieved to have escaped the interviewing process mostly unscathed, consulted his list of questions in the hope that it would provide some clue as to what he should do next.

CHAPTER 9

THE DINNER PARTY

In all the years Milton had lived at Radcliffe House, he had never hosted a party, nor attended one, as far as his neighbors knew. (As editor of *Toad in a Hole*, which faithfully reported such events, Lady Mariah would have made it her business to know.) He was not on bad terms with any of them, but rather, simply was not on any terms with them. He glided by on his walks and maintained a nodding acquaintance with whomever he met on his way, extending all the good manners anyone could ask, yet kept a distance from them, as though the chasm between him and his neighbors, if narrow, was unfathomably deep.

When Lady Mariah read the invitation to a dinner party at Radcliffe House to inaugurate the beginning of his expedition, a hunger stirred within her. She ran for Gerard, ran for her boa, ran for all her best party clothes, her heart racing faster than her feet.

"Why would he throw such a party?" Gerard wondered aloud on the evening in question. "After so many years of keeping to himself, why a party? And why now?"

"Just get ready, dear," said Lady Mariah. "We mustn't be late. Not for *this!*"

Lady Mariah hurried her husband into his frock coat and top hat, then bustled him into their coach, which rattled to a stop before Radcliffe House at seven o'clock precisely, so that their arrival was fiercely punctual. Upon presenting themselves at the door, they were admitted to the drawing room, where a few other guests awaited. Among the company: fellow expeditioner Mr. Crum, a reporter from *The Times,* and his wife.

Among the Radcliffe staff: two servants and an elderly butler hired at the last minute who had no idea where anything was, including their master, for which they made the most profuse and awk-ward apologies.

As they waited, Mr. Crum made a few attempts at polite conversation to which the others fol-lowed suit, but their words fell stark and small about their feet in the emptiness of the chamber. Since to sweep them up would only call attention to their failure, everyone returned to examining the room in silence, or in whispers.

This suited Lady Mariah just fine, as she was clearly more interested in either confirming or lay-ing to rest as many rumors as she could about Radcliffe House. She peered. She scrutinized. She made her rounds in the room, and even poked her head into other rooms, fishing for clues. Despite himself, Gerard began to wonder: Was it really the house of lost things?

Or was it something else?

There were no showy chandeliers, no stentorian balustrades, no elaborate rugs or glamorous vases. In fact, there wasn't much of anything. Many of the rooms were simply empty, and the ones that had any furnishings at all were quiet, quiet, quiet.

It was no accident that their voices had dropped to near whispers when they entered the house. Do you shout in a museum? Do you hoot and holler in a sanctuary? There was a mirror in the foyer. A venerable oaken face was carved in the mirror's frame—it was almost as if it were holding a finger to its lips, begging silence. It was as though every tome in the library were sleeping, as though every vase and bowl and misty window pane were made of eggshell. Everyone slowed, hushed, moved on tiptoe. It was a house of cards. A house of glass.

Lady Mariah made the mistake of looking down the west hall, where the old gallery lay in ruins, still.

When she returned, her face was pinched and white, the curiosity drained away. She drew Gerard aside and whispered into his ear.

"Let's not stay any longer than we absolutely must."

"Whatever do you mean? You've waited for an opportunity to see inside this house for years. Now that you're here, you want to go home? Isn't this your dream come true?"

"Gerard, it's awful. That gallery, all burnt and left rotting like that, and Mr. Radcliffe ignoring it as if nothing were wrong. Why do you suppose he doesn't do something? Why doesn't he set it to rights?"

Gerard ignored a sudden chill. "Let's not mention the gallery tonight, my dear. This is supposed to be a festive occasion."

"Then why do I feel as though we're here to pay our last respects?"

"Don't be ridiculous," said Gerard.

The others, too, had noticed the west wing, not because they saw it directly, but because they saw evidence of it: a little eddy of ash had blown in and scattered itself across the floor.

They saw it, but they ignored it.

They were in a house of wind. A house of ruin. A still-life, crusted in ancient oils.

Milton's house.

And gliding among it all without stirring a single dust mote, their immaculate host appeared as if from thin air.

He was dressed as he always was, the same silk cravat ruthlessly straight, the same crisp black suit, the same shoes polished mirror-bright.

He nodded graciously.

The tattered antique of a butler announced that dinner was served.

Glad to escape the drawing room, they all progressed to the dining hall, where they took their places at a table that tried to live up to the occasion amicably, but whose clumsy settings fell short of the mark. Gerard noticed at once that the silverware, for instance, did not match, and creases scarred the musty tablecloth. Still, everyone smiled and made what good cheer they could, decor notwithstanding.

It would have been customary at that point for their host to lead the conversation along some fruitful course. But when Milton's guests looked to him for that cue, he only looked back amicably, or off into the shadows of the room, or into his soup. After a few perfunctory pleasantries, the guests fell silent, so that the clinking of utensils in that dim hall began to become unbearable. Everyone smiled congenially at everyone else, everyone gingerly picked at their food (which, to Gerard's palate, tasted as though something terrible had happened in the kitchen), and everyone ventured little probing glances at Milton, almost as though each was afraid of getting caught, but no one could settle into conversation or, for that matter, into his or her seats. In addition to bearing the weight of the awful silence and the awful *clink, clink, clink* of the utensils, all the guests were distracted by their efforts to maintain the polite fiction that the draft gusting in from the west wing did not exist. Milton could see a nervousness in their faces. It was almost as though they expected the eddy of ashes to find them any minute, and whirl them away.

Gerard tried to start the thing. "You must be very excited, Mr. Radcliffe, to be on the brink of such an expedition. Do you feel you are well prepared?"

Looking up briefly, Milton said that he was, then returned his attention to his soup.

Eyes wandered nervously.

Again: "So, this journal you found, the Larking journal. What an extraordinary find! Would you favor us with the story of how you came across such a treasure?"

Milton said that he bought it.

Clink, clink, clink.

This time Lady Mariah: "You must have been so excited when you found the journal! You know I read the most interesting article in *Peterson's Pundit* about this Jonathan Larking. Tell us, Mr. Radcliffe, judging by what you've read in his journals, would you say he was as eccentric as they claim?" (This drew a sideways glance from Gerard: You are walking on dangerous ground here. Discuss madness with Radcliffe? Careful, my dear, careful!)

Milton said he didn't think so.

Mr. Crum to the rescue: He had read the journal quite thoroughly, and considered Mr. Larking to be a man of great genius, and asked if the present company would forgive them if he and his esteemed colleague seemed reticent about discussing the subject of the journal, which at this juncture (surely they must understand) must remain highly confidential.

They assured him that they understood, and Mr. Crum said he knew they would and smiled very agreeably, and all the nervous eyes flocked to him, leaving Milton to his meal.

From thereon in, the Reporter directed questions to Mr. Crum, evidently discerning him to be

Milton's right-hand man (and as such, the one appointed to do all the talking). Mr. Crum warmed up to this role nicely, and asserted with all ease that they were indeed prepared for their journey; that the two of them could make the full journey alone without assistance; that although his employer had never led such an expedition as this before, still he had every confidence in the leadership and skill of his esteemed colleague; that he was himself a patron of the arts, and had been ever since he was a boy; etc., etc.

When asked about his own experience on similar expeditions, Mr. Crum uncorked one tale after another. He led his company from the heart of the Black Forest to the fountains of Rome, through sundry twists and turns and feats of derring-do that had won him a reputation (if not in England, then at least abroad) as an expeditioner of the highest caliber, yes sir, if he could say it in all modesty, the very highest caliber. The longer he talked, the faster he talked, and the faster he talked, the further forward the Reporter leaned in his chair, and soon was on the very edge of his seat while Mr. Crum illustrated his tale with gestures and props recruited from the table service.

Whether Milton merely had nothing to contribute to the conversation, or whether he followed the conversation at all, was difficult to say. His eyes wandered throughout the evening, sometimes examining his food, sometimes gazing at one or another of his guests the way he might study a painting, sometimes looking at nothing at all. Inasmuch as Milton was present, he was polite. But something kept pulling him away, and he evidently responded to it more readily than he would to any of his visible guests.

Gerard began to suspect that Milton had invited them all merely to keep him company on a night that marked the end of something, a caterpillar's farewell party to the cocoon that had been its home all its life. Yet he also instinctively knew that Milton was himself oblivious to his own motives. Gerard imagined his host humming some old nursery rhyme to himself as he'd sealed the invitations.

No one mentioned the west wing, but no one could completely ignore it. It hung about them, with every draft that stole in from the hall in the corridor. The Reporter's wife darted uncomfortable glances in its direction. Perhaps unconsciously, the Reporter himself hugged his dinner coat as though he were testing its readiness to protect him from some imminent storm. Lady Mariah drew her boa around her neck to ward it off. The only two who seemed truly oblivious to its taunts were Mr. Crum (who was far too enthralled in his own tale to take notice) and Milton himself.

Gerard felt the draft swirling around the table, toying with the candles, touching him. Though he was duty-bound to stay, he could not help but begin scheming up excuses to leave early. Throughout the rest of the evening, the excuses piled up in the back of his mind, and he held on to the better ones, that they might save him in a pinch, should those ashes come for him after all.

During the ride home, Lady Mariah looked at the window, and did not speak. Not until they arrived home and settled in their warm, quiet drawing room did she finally let out what she had held in all evening long.

"Gerard, someone must stop that poor man!"

Gerard frowned. "What would you suggest we do? Turn him in to an asylum?"

Lady Mariah shivered at the word *asylum*. "I don't know what to do. I only know that something must be done. We can't let him go."

"You speak of him as though he were a child," said Gerard.

No sooner had he said it than he regretted saying it. It recalled to him a single instant when he had met Milton's eyes during the course of dinner. Looking at him then, did he not see the boy inside the man? Didn't he see that Milton was filled to the brim with nothing but orphan's nursery rhymes and nursery games? Wasn't the whole expedition nothing more than a game of marbles to him? A colossal round of blind-man's-bluff? And wasn't Milton the blindfolded one, amusedly groping at the sky, yet straying away from the game altogether, losing himself further with every step? If he failed to tag his playmate, he might totter on like that for miles, and for years. Who would have the heart, then, to tell him his field was empty? Even if someone did, would Milton hear?

CHAPTER 10

THE RETURN OF
THULEMANDER

He was Milton Radcliffe, traveler, explorer. His world was immense. He traveled everywhere, through every part of the shire, every day. As soon as he rose, his journey began. He awoke in the town of Bedchamber and, upon rising, visited the neighboring wilderness of Tub, wherein he swam in a great lake. There he would soak himself soggy, and not emerge until the tips of his fingers shriveled into prunes, after which he would rise up into the crisp dawn and return to the land. Adjacent to Tub was Wardrobe, a tailor's town, wherein he adorned himself in lavish costume, and assembled his equipment for his journey (handkerchief and a tin of sweets, always). From Wardrobe it was a short walk to the quiet hamlet of Kitchen, where the ripest pippins spilled forth from tremendous bowls, and the freshest eggs popped and sputtered musically in great black frying pans. He feasted heartily, for he knew his journey would be long.

His itinerary took him next to Study, the center of commerce, where he walked through the vast archives of public records and sometimes sat at a great desk to dispatch his own fiscal affairs with a great quill pen. He occasionally took a brief detour through Rumpus or Billiard, though both those counties had degenerated ages ago into slums. By midday he would reach Dining Hall, a town of great pomp and splendor, where again he would feast, then take a brief sojourn to neighboring Den, teacup in hand, and prepare for the final leg of his journey.

Milton the Traveler! Milton the Wayfarer! Milton the Pilgrim, the Captain, the Nomad! Watch him go!

He was now very close to Museum.

Museum, City of Cities.

Castle-high corridors, stretching for miles! Golden-paned windows looking in on other worlds! And through one particular portal he would venture to a strange and beautiful land. . . .

When he returned from Museum, he took the main road back, which led to a great crossroads, Library.

One day, he had seen Lord Tennyson slumped before a desk, staring out the window, searching the meadow for inspiration. The next, Blake freshly thunderstruck, blazing pen across paper in a fit. Always excitement in Library, always a spectacle. Milton had met the finest company in that grand forum, and learned many lessons from them, and marveled at their ways.

It was an idyllic life. A life of adventure.

Sometimes he traveled even farther, to the farthest pinnacles of the known world.

Bakery Pass, where the best loaves of sourdough yeasted up in warm domes. The rocky crags of Sutter Street, far to the north. The plains of Cambridge Park. And perhaps the most exotic of all, the far-flung Isle of Tussaud, where the celebrities of a dozen ages had retreated to found their own colony, and, as was the custom of that strange community, wrapped themselves in a living sleep. Milton walked among the tableaux, careful not to wake them, reading the stories they depicted, like legends frozen in pantomime.

Milton, then, was a man of the world. He had seen much, and traveled far. If anyone had asked him to describe his adventures, he had a wealth of fabric from which to weave his tale. But there was one land which he would never have been able to describe, the farthest and strangest land of all. Behind a secret rosewood panel, Milton had hidden the one world he had traversed more than any other, the only frontier he had never fully explored: Larking Land. His greatest expedition, he knew, would be his trek up Thistle River, to discover its source.

Soon, he would return.

Down through the mint patch, down through the dockweed, down through the bed of bluebells, to the blue-white river . . .

Soon.

The night before the expedition he snuggled himself in his reading chair in the library, and he began to doze off into a grogginess that was not quite sleep. Every now and again his eyelids would droop, and his chin would sink to his chest, and his book would settle into his lap. Then he'd rouse himself.

Just a few more minutes, he would think, and begin to read again.

He kept reading the same passage, over and over.

Read, doze, rouse. Read, doze, rouse. . . .

The house was dark except for the globe of light from the single lamp by which he read. Its flame wavered lazily, swaying shadows. His eyelids felt heavy.

It was no use.

He had thought the book would help.

It didn't. He awoke again, or half awoke.

He looked at the page, the same page.

It had changed.

Where the page had been filled with text, it now bore a single message:

Beyond This Point There Abide Dragons

Handwritten in tall, hooked letters.

Milton shook his head, rubbed his eyes, looked at the page again.

And the message was gone. It was the same old page again, with the same old text.

But he was not fooled. He knew what had happened, and he knew who was behind it. He was wide awake now. He snapped the book shut, and scanned the darkness suspiciously.

Don't you dare come back now. Not now.

The flame in the globe danced and diminished. The shadows weaved. The hairs rose on the back of his neck, sensing each shifting draft. He listened, yet heard no sound but his own pulse beating, a little faster now.

Leave me alone.

A visitor stood at the library entrance, tall, robed, unmoving. The Sea of Darkness, Milton thought, and he knew it was all coming back.

"Thank goodness I've reached you in time," the visitor said, and glided toward Milton, who shrank back.

Thulemander.

Although Milton looked away, he could feel where Thulemander stopped, just on the shore where darkness lapped on his guttering island of lamplight, just on the edge where everything was shadow and vapor. He could feel eyes probing him, reading him.

"You heard it last night, didn't you?" Thulemander asked.

Milton didn't answer.

"I came to warn you."

Milton stared coldly into his book, without reading. He stared a long time. But Thulemander was patient.

"Do you think that if you ignore it long enough, it will go away? Is that how you plan to win? How many times has it paid you a visit in the last month, Milton? A dozen times? A score? Two score? Has it come every night?"

A page shivered in Milton's hand as he turned it blindly.

"I've brought you something," his visitor said, and produced a large, dusty tome. Milton kept to his own book, and dared not look up.

"The *New Cosmographie*," Thulemander said significantly.

New? thought Milton. The *New Cosmographie?*

"The second edition," continued Thulemander. "There are some additions in here I think will interest you. At least, they should."

Though Milton refused to look at the tremendous book held before him, his eye could not help but wander back to the far shelf where his first edition of the arcane tome rested, again gathering dust.

"I understand you intend to launch an expedition to find Lorien. I also understand that you believe her to be waiting for you somewhere in the land of Devonshire, yes? Well, my friend, Devonshire is a long ways away. It is much farther than you think. It is much farther than *I* thought when I drew up the maps for the first edition."

Milton's blood ran cold.

"Have you started packing yet, Milton? Plenty of preparations to be made for a journey as long as yours. Horses. Provisions. Lanterns. Oil. Guns."

A brief glance at Milton, who turned a shade paler.

"You do plan to take muskets, don't you? Have you ever fired a musket, Milton? No? How curious. How very very odd. A man who has never fired a musket, never camped on the moors, never sailed on any kind of vessel, never gone a day without a meal, never even ventured farther than ten miles from his own home, where he has lived all his life, suddenly decides to lead an expedition. My, how very enterprising you've become, Milton! How very enterprising indeed. Now tell me: What do you plan to do when you venture out there looking for Lorien, and instead you find a basilisk? Do you know what a basilisk is, Milton?"

His pupil was speechless.

"A basilisk is a kind of Dragon that lives in the remote regions of the world, in rocky crags, whose gaze will turn men to stone. On a trip to Middleham I traveled through Knaresborough, where I found dozens of men gathered at the entrance to a cave—men who had been turned to stone. They were all averting their eyes from something that had come from inside the cave. They had turned away too late, of course. Pilgrims, Visigoths, Saxons, knights, all petrified from a single creature's gaze. You should have seen the look that was captured on their faces."

Though Milton closed his eyes, he could not escape the image Thulemander had conjured of petrified travelers cringing from some absent horror, strewn across the landscape like derelict chessmen.

"Have you ever heard of a wyvern? Wyverns are quite a sight: the body of a serpent, the wings of a bat, the legs of an eagle. Their mere breath carries pestilence upon it, and some say it was the wyverns that spread the Plague throughout England.

"I believe I've told you that Dragons are even more intelligent than men? No one knows what powers a Dragon might have. There is a Dragon named Gierwurm who lives in a cave in the mountains of Northumbria, who lures his prey into his lair with mirages of treasures that vanish only after he's ensnared them. He's a wily one, this Gierwurm. Who knows the extent of *his* powers? I'm told that different people will see different treasures. Can he also read minds, then, this Gierwurm?"

Milton heard the creaking roofbeams from the night before whispering now in his ear.

"Can he read *your* mind, Milton?"

Thulemander began to pace, warming to his inquiry. He waved a hand demonstratively to the walls.

"Suppose he can. What treasure would he use to lure you? Well, it would be easy, wouldn't it? You see a pavilion. It's lush, splendid. You run to it without thinking, without hesitation. You find a woman inside, the most beautiful woman you've ever seen. Ah, she's beautiful, isn't she? The very woman you've searched for. You've found Lorien! Oh, indeed!"

Thulemander laughed. "Isn't that marvelous? Your quest is at an end—and so down you go trundling off into Gierwurm's lair, blissful and oblivious. 'And no one ever heard or saw the likes of Milton Radcliffe ever again!'"

Milton saw the Northumbrian mountains, heard a hot-bellowed breath simmer up from some dark stone throat deep within them.

"What do you suppose that is, Milton? What has come to visit us? A manticore? A griffin? A gargoyle, flown all the way from the Isle of Wight? Or do you suppose it might be some creature we've never seen before? Some new fellow that has eluded my bestiary?"

Yellow eyes, moss-green eyes, membraned eyes, a dozen lidless eyes stared at Milton. Webbed fingers tugged at his shirt sleeve. Talons softly pricked the arm of his chair. But Milton did not flinch.

"An excellent time to find out," suggested Thulemander, eyeing the ceiling.

Without standing up, Milton managed to scoot his chair around to face away from his guest.

"There he is! Look, everybody—Milton, the great explorer! Let's all rally around!"

"Leave me alone!" blurted Milton. "I'm not going that far. I'm only going to Devonshire, not World's End. I won't even leave land."

Thulemander descended on him, gripped the arms of Milton's chair, and pinned him with a piercing look. "You fool! Listen to me. That is exactly what I came here to warn you about: I was *wrong* when I drew up the first edition of my *Cosmographie*. I've learned much since then, from travelers, and from my own explorations. The World's End is much closer than you think. It's much closer than *I* thought. You are living very close to the Edge, dangerously close! *That* is why the Dragons come here to perch on your roof at night. Do you think I came here to mock you? I came here to save you from a danger you clearly don't understand. They've chosen this site as their next foothold, and they're waiting for you to come out."

Milton had clapped his hands over his ears.

"You don't think that fire was really caused by a faulty gas lamp, do you? They struck the heart of your collection. They destroyed your portal to Larking Land to strand you here, because they knew that would lure you out. Care to play into their hands? Go ahead, step outside!"

Milton squeezed his eyelids tight and tried to shut out the terrible sound that had returned to haunt the rooftop just two short nights before.

"Listen to me: I have drawn new charts, new maps. They appear in the new edition, but even these are incomplete. A more experienced traveler might have a better chance—"

"Get out!" cried Milton. "Leave me alone!"

Thulemander laughed a long dark laugh that was filled with pity.

"Oh, aren't you a sight! A babe in the woods!

"Milton, do you remember when you were a young boy, how you used to play in the land surrounding this estate? Right out there," Thulemander said, pointing out the window. "You'd never go very far, would you? Why was that?"

Don't look him in the eye. Just don't look him in the eye.

"You would run to your room and hide in your bed, beneath the sheets. What were you hiding from?"

You know what it was. You know. And you've brought it back, to spoil everything. I'm not going to look. I'm not going to look into your eyes, and I'm not going to give in. I'll find a way somehow. I'll find a way to go out there but I'm not going to tell you anything, because you'll twist it somehow, anything I tell you you'll twist and ruin.

But not even silence was safe. Thulemander tasted the silence, and found it sweet. He savored it, and Gierwurm's forked tongue tested the air, and the lidless eyes still studied Milton. He could feel them watching him from all sides.

"Good luck," rasped Thulemander.

Milton did not open his eyes until he was sure Thulemander was gone.

"There's nothing out there," he said to himself. "*It* hasn't come back." But he would not look out the window.

Milton had discovered the book in the library when he was nine.

He had educated himself by reading one antiquated volume after another in the mansion library. He had explored Ancient Greece. He had visited Rome. And one day, he had cracked open a great compendium whose title page announced:

COSMOGRAPHIE
Being a Faithful Translation of the Original 1304 Edition
by the Mysterious Scholar and Cartographer
Thulemander of Wessex

Copiously illustrated with charts, diagrams, and maps, *Cosmographie* depicted the world as a flat disk, with a single landmass called Eurasia surrounded by a single body of water, Oceanus. In the middle of Eurasia lay civilization: cities, abbeys, castles. The outer regions became less densely populated, and more wild. Travel too far north, and you might encounter wolves. Too far south, boars. Travel too deeply into wilderness and you might tangle into a web of giant spiders, or sink into a bog glistening with toothy adders.

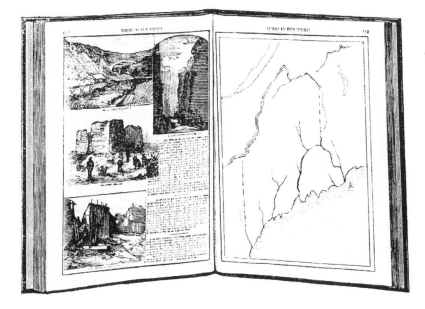

Thulemander had mapped out the different winds, the currents, the common trade routes, all very meticulous and detailed, all sure and unmistakable. He had labeled the major cities, various mountain ranges, and smaller inland seas and their ports. He had even drawn a representative or two from each region, dressed in the garb of their land. A stout Spartan raised a sword. A robed and bearded Greek lectured the sky. Green waves indicated Oceanus. The farther away from shore, the more dangerous the waters became, until they teemed with all manner of sea serpents and ship-rending monsters (all illustrated in *Cosmographie*'s bestiary), and finally extended to the very Edge of the World. This farthest frontier of the Earth itself simply fell off into oblivion, a black void which Thulemander called the Sea of Darkness. He described it as a limitless night that marked the end of all things.

Young Milton had examined the map carefully, his eye roaming over the waters. If he listened closely, he could hear the waves spill into nothingness at the far rim of Oceanus. He could hear them fall, but he could never hear them hit bottom.

Thulemander had written a single admonition in the far margin, the words hovering over Oceanus as a final warning to all seafarers so foolish or so far lost as to have strayed from known waters:

Beyond This Point There Abide Dragons

And below the words he had drawn one of the beasts, writhing in the mist and snapping at the air.

According to Thulemander's bestiary, the Dragons had originated from the Sea of Darkness, and were slowly encroaching on the civilized world. The Dragons, he wrote, possessed intelligence, as well as mysterious powers. Being creatures of chaos, they hated the ordered world of humanity, and had devised a scheme to overrun their enemy's stronghold by a war of attrition, capturing a mountain pass here, a strategic cave there, invading first remote hamlets, then moving slowly inward to scorch the towns and cities one by one, until the whole of mankind would be toasted in their cinder breath, and the world would be theirs.

The Dragons, warned Thulemander, were closing in.

Young Milton used to play in the land surrounding the Radcliffe estate, and on those nights when the fog rolled in and erased the trees and obscured the horizon, he stopped short amid its coldness, and he knew that if he ran much farther into that blind landscape, he could not tell where the world ended and the long cold falling began. If he listened closely, he could hear the beating of leathery wings, vast as a galleon's sails, drumming through the hills, and he knew the Edge must be much closer than Thulemander had supposed. He would freeze and listen to his heart race, and run home.

On rainy nights, he would lay in bed and listen, and swear he could hear some great lumbering weight land on the rooftop, followed by the sound of giant talons clenching the roofbeam. On those nights he hid beneath the sheets, held his breath, and didn't make a sound until he thought the beast had flown away, or until he fell asleep in a tight little ball.

The Edge of the World must be very close, thought young Milton, for the Dragons to perch on my roof at night.

He preferred to stay indoors, and read.

Even now, there were some nights when the rafters still creaked and, without thinking, Milton's hand stopped before the doorknob, and he thought better of venturing outside. Instead he would hang up his coat, retreat to his warm, quiet library, and disappear into some musty book. There were many nights like that, and even during the day when some unavoidable business drew him out of Radcliffe House and into the great outer world, he never went beyond these boundaries: the Mariah estate to the north, the Thames to the south, the Grosmont Art Gallery to the east, Madame Tussaud's Waxworks to the west.

CHAPTER 11

THE EXPEDITION
LAUNCHED

Mr. Crum shrugged on his Mackintosh and galoshes and marched out into the drizzle the next morning. His overshoes squeaked in the slick grass, and the mist collected on the brim of his hat in tiny pearls. Milton held the journal tight.

He watched from a fogged window. The coach, Mr. Crum, and the whole hillside appeared shimmering and frosty, and somehow very distant. When Mr. Crum called his name, it sounded as if it came from miles away.

He picked up his last traveling bag and looked back at the hall one last time.

"Devonshire is not so far," he told himself.

How do you know?

What? Did he hear something? From the library, the faintest whisper of pages? The softest creak of an arcane tome opening, mumbling its secrets?

Don't go, don't go.

He left, closing the door tight behind him.

He did not look back at Radcliffe House as he walked away from it toward the coach.

The expedition party was ready to go. Mr. Crum had already assumed his post atop the coach box, and was presently testing the reins of a spirited horse. Gerard and Lady Mariah had arrived to see them off (Lady Mariah complete with astrakhan muff and an elaborate hat whose plumage faintly wilted in the drizzle). A round of handshakes and best wishes. Mr. Crum cracked the reins. The expedition had begun.

Milton sat below inside the coach, looking out the window. Only now that the vehicle was in motion and past the point of no return did he allow himself to look back. He watched Radcliffe House receding in the distance, and now the house looked shimmering and frosty, as if it were disappearing behind a sheet of water. He turned his attention to the road up ahead, which was swallowed by the fogbank.

It can't be that far, thought Milton.

But everything in his world was disappearing. Radcliffe House drowned in a watery veil behind him, and up ahead, he saw his familiar walk appear, then vanish from view. Every lamp post that he knew by heart faded and dissolved away into nothing, and for the first time he realized that he did not know when he would see those kindly sentinels again. He wanted to cry out to them and beckon them to follow. *Come with me,* he thought. *Protect me. Burn through the white barrier and clear me a path.* He watched the familiar landscape drip away behind him, and he began to wonder what he had done.

What happens to a place when you leave it? worried Milton. Does it go on the same, just as though I was there? Will it all stop like a photograph, or a still-life caught in oil? Or will it miss me? Will the sentinels come looking for me, lamping the darkness to make rounds through coppery side streets and narrow alleys, inquiring of the shop signs and hitching posts, where I might have gone?

All these thoughts tossed and turned in Milton's mind while he stared out of the back window of the coach as it rambled slowly down a road that was funeral quiet, and nearly empty.

Will it all be there when I return?

He stopped looking back.

* * *

The coach trundled down the road, disappearing into the sea of fog. Gerard thought how that was very much like Milton, always disappearing in a mist, inscrutably. He stared at Radcliffe House, particularly the ruins of the west wing, and he wondered what happens to a house that loses its ghost. Does it fold up like an accordion and vanish? Does it call to its master in rafter sighs and roofbeam groans, begging him to return? Does it finally surrender itself to the cobwebs and beetles and the sands of time that have dusted its halls, encroaching by imperceptible degrees year after year, and settle into its own earthly sleep? Or does it merely wait? Gerard searched for the answer in the quiet facade of Radcliffe House, but the building, as mysterious as ever, revealed nothing.

A thought troubled him. The same thought must have been troubling Lady Mariah, who blurted it out.

"I wonder if this is the last time we will ever see Milton Radcliffe," she said.

"Hmph!" said Gerard, and beckoned her to their carriage, and off they went.

CHAPTER 12

PLACKETT MANOR

"Steady as she goes!" cried Mr. Crum agreeably from his high vantage point. "Sure you don't care to join me atop here and take in the view, Mr. Radcliffe? Plenty to see. Plenty of fresh air."

"No, thank you," shouted Milton from within the coach.

He preferred to read his correspondence.

Milton had so preoccupied himself with last-minute preparations that he had forgotten the single letter that had been delivered him before he'd left. Only now did he retrieve the envelope from his greatcoat pocket and frown at the unfamiliar name, Adrian Plackett. He opened it, puzzled.

Dear Mr. Radcliffe:

   Having read your advertisement in The Times *regarding your proposed expedition to recover the statue created in secret by Mr. Jonathan Larking, I would like to discuss with you a matter of business. As an art collector myself, I appreciate the value of your most amazing discovery, and would like to make a proposal to you regarding it that I feel certain would engage your interest. I would prefer to discuss the details of this proposal with you in person, as a matter of confidence, at my estate at your earliest convenience. While I understand the urgency of your own schedule, concerning this matter I wish to discuss, time is essential.*

                                                    Most Respectfully,
                                                    Adrian Plackett, Esq.

The note concluded with Mr. Plackett's address. Milton ventured to hand the letter out to Mr. Crum with the instruction that they alter their present course to visit the Plackett estate.

   The detour was not far out of their way, and the property was not easy to miss. A large, perfectly symmetrical manor house sat atop perfectly symmetrical grounds, the main attraction of which was a perfectly symmetrical formal garden, in which everything had been measured and cropped and cut and pruned and preened into a rigorous order. Each shrub was trimmed to geometric perfection. Each tulip and iris had grown to its prescribed height, and no taller. The stones were aligned ruler-steady in the walk. Not a single stray leaf or twig invaded the paths. The garden boasted every fashionable accessory, from a broad Grecian titan who looked oddly uncomfortable holding a sundial, to a fountain which almost seemed to resent trickling its neat little rivulets into a spotless alabaster basin; but it lacked the popular birdbath, Milton speculated, because there probably was no practical way to crop and trim the birds, and keep them where *they* belonged. There was a place for everything, and everything was in its place.

   Milton instructed Mr. Crum to mind the coach while he himself called on Mr. Plackett. With a smooth and careful step Milton made his way up the path to the front door, to be met by the first thing on the premises that was at odds with its surroundings.

   The door was answered by a faded Toy Soldier who had been left in the shop window too long, and had been bleached nearly colorless by the sun. His liveries were faded. His face was faded. And except for a certain crispness to his gait and a resentful resignation that hunched his shoulders, his whole person seemed eminently faded.

"Do you have an appointment?" he voiced in a fearful monotone.

"I'm sorry, I don't. Not exactly, anyway. I do have this letter. Mr. Plackett requested to see me at my earliest convenience."

The footman examined the letter with an air of boredom, requested Milton's card, examined it with equal boredom, and turned back inside the door. "This way," he said over his shoulder, and led Milton into the manor's interior.

The drawing room was well lit, well polished, well swept, well dusted, and cluttered nearly to claustrophobic density, despite its immense size. The floor was covered with furniture, the walls with paintings. Bonington nearly bumped into Vermeer. Roman vineyards almost encroached onto Spanish ports. The pieces of furniture similarly competed with each other, but never quite stepped on each other, because all had been policed by a set of invisible rulers. Milton could see the lines that ran throughout every arrangement where enormous measuring tapes must have been strung to guide everything and snap it into place. (The only unruly section was a Diorama of statuettes, which looked sadly jumbled.)

"I will notify Mr. Plackett of your arrival," said the Toy Soldier, and marched off.

Milton remained standing for some time, worried that in taking a seat and inadvertently scooting it in any direction he might upset the harmony of the drawing room. Not until he had waited for some time, and inspected (without touching) a variety of pristine and fancy knickknacks on display all around him did he dare to sit, more out of exhaustion than daring.

Vases. Ewers. Ornamental urns. A row of fine china plates on display on a shelf that ran the length of the frieze at precise intervals, like targets in a shooting gallery. In front of him on an Italianate table, a golden snuff box. Several other snuff boxes, very ornate. How much snuff can one man snuff? thought Milton. Plenty, evidently.

A mantel clock ticked.

The fireplace, he noticed, was spotless.

Milton began to wonder if he had been forgotten. His eye continued to wander, and soon *he* began to wander, first merely to examine assorted items within the drawing room, then, furtively, to examine adjacent rooms. The paintings were not confined to the drawing room or the hall. They lined every available wall of every room. Although he found nothing by Jonathan Larking, he did find a dizzying assemblage of masters lined up rank-and-file nearly everywhere he looked. They all fought for his attention, so that before he could choose and really look at any one, another would catch his eye, until he had walked a mesmerized zigzag through several rooms and past a hundred glittering frames without having really seen anything. His head ached. And now he was lost.

His palms began to sweat.

He had never realized that he had a poor sense of direction because he had never needed one. Now that he was lost, he realized just how lost he was. After retracing his steps in several different directions, he debated whether he should continue his fruitless search for the drawing room or call for the Toy Soldier, surrender himself as a trespasser, and face the consequences. He had just parted his lips when he heard a muffled voice shouting from somewhere upstairs. Though he could not make out the words, the voice ranted venomously, as though it were threatening violence. Milton froze.

A pound, as that of a fist on a table. Every plate and vase in Plackett Manor rattled.

Milton scuttled off in a new direction.

Down one corridor. Down another. The halls grew darker and more austere. The farther he went the darker they became, until he had nearly left daylight behind. The somber wood paneling gave way to walls that were painted to resemble porphyry, and blended with the shadows, so he could not tell where the walls ended and the shadows began. A few dim shafts of light filtered through stained, leaded windows to cast dim pools onto a host of statues that huddled in the darkness. They reminded Milton of a painting he had seen of a medieval dungeon, where the prisoners had been rag-doll-tossed into the earthy depths in manacles, and as he scanned the darkness, he could not be certain he didn't see stone vassals and poachers shackled in dank mobs all around him. A marble peasant in that corner, begging mercy? Over there, a thief?

He passed a bust of a severe man who might have been a judge casting a guilty verdict at the instant the sculptor had raised his chisel. The dim light cast straight down upon it to elongate the features into something grotesque: a judge-turned-gargoyle.

Milton spied something glinting in the gloom ahead. A doorknob.

An escape?

He eased it open.

Paintings. Hundreds of them.

Maybe thousands. They were not on display, but actually stacked atop each other in small towers that piled up as tall as Milton, in row after row that extended as far as he could see. He reeled at the number, a number beyond any ledger.

(What happens to paintings deprived of light? Do they yellow like the grass beneath old boards? Do they pale like fish raised in sunless waters?)

He walked among the towers.

The stale air had suggested to his lungs that the room might be smaller than it turned out to be. The rows took him for a maze walk that lost him still further. Had he been concerned about finding his way back, he might have panicked, but his thoughts turned toward the great hoard instead. He found a candlestick and a tinderbox, lit the candle, and continued.

He inspected the top painting of each stack, gently blowing to remove a layer of dust obscuring it. Beneath each little cloud-squall that he created across each canvas plain, he saw faces, landscapes, stories.

Lorien, are you in here?

A vineyard. A pier. A flaking parlor.

Lorien, can you hear me? Are you in here? I'll keep looking.

A dusk-sunk village. A little girl cradling a cat.

I just want to go back. I just want to see the oats again, and the light of Lampyridae's lamp shining through them. I want to see Thistle River.

A dust storm churned. Below it, a coach tilted through a milling street. Under another, a consort of black-frocked guildsmen prepared to brave a starless night.

I'll find the window. I'll find it any minute, and I'll leap through and leave this place behind.

He tripped in the gloom, regained his footing. The globe of light shrank by slow degrees, darkness eroding it in slow tides.

I must be so close. I'll find you, and run through the Oat Field, only this time I will run forever. I'll keep running and running and I'll never go back.

The candle trembled, and with it wavered a host of phantom shadows.

Carefully, gently, he began lifting the top paintings to peek at those below. An orchard bloomed beneath the dust of one, but he could barely make it out. As the candle guttered and the dust thickened, the places blurred into obscurity. He pored over their surfaces, blew, squinted hard, a miner searching for gold.

Where are you, Lorien? Say something. Give me a sign. You must be here, because I need you to be here now, I need a way out of this place. I can't stay here.

Searching, one after another, through stack after stack after stack . . .

He moved the wrong painting. A pool of spiders poured over the floor. Several climbed up his arm. He refused to acknowledge them any more than to brush them off.

Lorien, do you remember that day we all chased you in the field? It's funny: I can almost smell the wild grasses right now. If I could only smell that smell again . . . I never should have left that day. I don't know why I did. I don't remember. But I never should have left. I should have stayed there, where I belong. I'm coming back. As soon as I find you, I'm coming back.

His candle was very nearly out.

He moved a little more quickly now as he hunted through one stack after another of the great gold frames piled up like so much dry firewood.

Another spider skittered over his hand. He brushed it off.

I'm on my way.

He had searched until he had exhausted himself without finding any window into Larking Land. He did not know how long he had stumbled through that dark keep before he found his way back to the main floor to discover that the Toy Soldier had returned, looking as though he had been stripped of his rank. Although he still wore the faded liveries, his resentful hunch had sunken to a humiliated slouch, and his gait, though still crisp, was shaken.

"My master says I am to apologize to you, sir, for keeping you waiting so long," droned the Toy Soldier from under a dejected scowl. "I do apologize, sir. Mr. Plackett will see you now."

He led Milton through a maze of halls to a tremendous paneled door, opened it noiselessly. Within, a tall, broad man in a frock coat and top hat stood before a tremendous painting, waving a slender cane ringmaster-style and shouting at the high-wire act that balanced atop a tottering ladder.

"Crooked!" the large man shouted. "Do you call that straight? It's crooked!"

"But Mr. Plackett, I've measured with the string very precisely, just like you said—"

"I don't trust your string and your measuring! I trust my eye! I know a crooked painting when I see one!"

The high-wire performer lost her courage. She blanched. She slackened the line of string she had run across the frame-tops, looking at it imploringly. The ringmaster shook his head.

"Crooked!"

The Toy Soldier bellowed: "*Mister* Radcliffe!" to no one in particular. Milton jumped. The high-wire performer nearly toppled from her perch.

Having made his announcement, and thus discharged his duty, the footman slouched away. The ringmaster snapped around to greet Milton.

He wore a virgin snowy ascot and a watery grin. His top hat was freshly steamed.

"A pleasure to meet you, Mr. Radcliffe. A pleasure I'm sure!"

He wrung Milton's hand enthusiastically.

"I'm sorry the footman kept you waiting."

"It was no trouble, really."

Mr. Plackett offered some pleasantries about Milton's trip and how glad he was to see Milton and how fortuitous it was that he had replied so promptly, all of which were lost on Milton, who was distracted by the tremendous painting. No matter how hard he looked, he could find not the slightest skew. The frame was absolutely, flawlessly straight.

"Allow me to give you a brief tour of my collection—"

"No, no!" fumbled Milton. "I've—that is, I'm rather short of time."

"Ah, a busy man, I'm sure. Let's get down to business then, shall we?"

"Yes. Let's."

With that, they retired to Mr. Plackett's accounting room. Mr. Plackett took his seat of authority behind a tremendous desk, an open ledger spread before him.

Business was simple: He had read Milton's advertisement in *The Times,* and had a particular interest in the Larking statue. Mr. Plackett was not an expeditioner, but wished to hire a team to recover the sculpture. Mr. Plackett wanted to know what Mr. Radcliffe intended to do with the item, if he might ask?

Milton stammered something about adding it to his private collection.

Mr. Plackett inquired if Mr. Radcliffe was in the particular business of collecting works of art; that is, in the *business* of buying and selling them?

Milton stated that he supposed that was the case.

Mr. Plackett smiled with the sort of fondness of one who has found a companion. "I'm glad to find another as sensible as yourself in these matters, Mr. Radcliffe. I so often meet muddle-headed dreamers who get all swept up in the poetry of things, and forget that when we come down to brass tacks" (here he tapped his ledger significantly), "we are in a business. Oh, the poetry is fine. I've no trouble with that. But you and I are businessmen. We have business to conduct today. And I do not wish to waste your time."

Mr. Plackett's itchy finger produced a pen and checkbook. He suddenly became very grave.

"I have a great interest in the Larking statue, and am prepared to offer you what I think you will find to be a very fair sum, to be paid upon its delivery to my estate. Furthermore, I am willing to offer an additional sum to finance your expedition, to be refunded only if you fail to produce the Larking sculpture."

Milton knew he was about to fail another exam. He didn't know the right answer, and didn't know how to cheat. He stalled for time.

Mr. Plackett inquired if Mr. Radcliffe would like a drink of water?

No thank you, said Milton, both to the water and to the offer. Thank you very much, but he really wasn't interested.

Now at this point, something happened to Mr. Plackett's face. It looked like a cake that had fallen. It sort of caved in, all lumpy.

Milton knew that he had really muddled it this time, and that expulsion was imminent, but he would be glad to be dismissed, if only to escape from the dreary accountant's den and the collapsed expression of Mr. Plackett and the decaying rubbish heap of imprisoned paintings below.

But the test was not over. Not yet.

The cake made a feeble attempt to patch its surface with a little icing. It didn't work. The words were sugared, but the lumps still shone through.

"Well, surely you would at least like to hear my sum?"

Milton said he thought he might.

"One hundred thousand pounds," declared Mr. Plackett significantly.

Milton thanked him for his very generous offer, but still demurred.

The cake had fallen beyond salvation, but Mr. Plackett apparently didn't know it, because he kept smearing icing that wouldn't stick: Would Mr. Radcliffe care to take a day or two to think it over and perhaps reconsider? If he didn't mind his asking, did Mr. Radcliffe have any other interested parties approach him, with comparable sums, perhaps? Was Mr. Radcliffe at liberty to discuss any agreements with said parties that he might have made? Did Mr. Radcliffe simply find the sum too modest?

No.

Mr. Plackett sighed. Mr. Plackett shook his head ruefully, and smiled, as if at some old joke that he had heard too many times.

"You are a businessman, indeed," he said, opening his checkbook. He began to write. Milton started to stammer and object before the check was finished, but to no avail. Mr. Plackett handed him a sum much larger than the one he had quoted.

"I'm willing to pay you this in advance. Use it as you see fit. Buy whatever provisions you need, hire whomever you like to assist you in your expedition. Deliver the statue to me and I will pay you twice that amount, as the balance."

As Mr. Plackett pushed the check toward him with some emphasis, Milton shrank away from it.

"I'm sorry, Mr. Plackett. I'm sorry to have wasted your time. Your offer is very generous—please understand that I'm very grateful—but I just can't accept. I can't explain it, really, but I just can't accept. I'm very sorry."

Having made his plea for clemency, he awaited his verdict, no longer concerned with passing or failing (for he had sealed his fate there), but merely aching to be dismissed. Mr. Plackett, however, apparently did not understand. He studied Milton with some care, and the lumpiness of his face shifted in horrible ways that gave no hint to what he was thinking (though he clearly wasn't pleased), until it finally settled into a sort of resigned perplexity. He left the check in front of Milton, studied him, eyed the check as if to remind Milton that it was still there, studied Milton some more, then, seeing that this bait would not attract even a nibble, reluctantly withdrew it. He apologized to Milton for wasting *his* time, returned to the work of his ledger, and curtly bid him adieu.

The Toy Soldier awaited him at the door. Milton bowed profusely on his way out, and had one foot out of the den when Mr. Plackett made a parting request.

"Should you reconsider," he said without looking up from his ledger, "I will pay any sum you care to name."

"I'm terribly, terribly sorry," said Milton, and dashed for the main door, beating the footman to it.

CHAPTER 13

THE VOYAGE OF
CAPTAIN TARK

The expedition continued, now well out of London and into the countryside, toward Andover.

Milton left all the details to Mr. Crum. Mr. Crum plotted the itinerary. Mr. Crum had studied the journal very thoroughly, and employed his skill as an expeditioner of the very highest caliber to decipher the clues it gave, such as descriptions of the local flora and fauna, the weather and, most importantly, any references to roads, towns, or landmarks, any inferences indicating their distance or direction. He had done a great deal of homework on this journal without any prompting from Milton, and felt certain he knew precisely where the pavilion lay. Yet whenever Milton asked him, he grew vast and vague. "To the south," he would say, or, "In the countryside." How far? He did not give an estimate. Instead, he gave a list of reasons why estimates were impossible. Road conditions, weather conditions, the grade of the hills, the stamina and temperament of their horses, availability of shelter. The list went on and on, and in hearing it, Milton gained an appreciation for the experience and foresight of his fellow expeditioner. He would listen attentively until the road required Mr. Crum's attention, when he would leave him to his driving and return to his thoughts, or the scenery, or a book.

Milton felt fortunate. The journey would not be so difficult after all. He could dismiss all matters of timetables and geography to his partner, and enjoy the trip.

They stopped on the outskirts of Andover for the night.

Milton saw to the rooms. Mr. Crum saw to the coach.

This expeditioning business is not as harrowing as I expected, thought Milton as he retired. In fact, it's rather pleasant. He fluffed his pillow, sank into it, watched the scenery roll by again on the ceiling until he fell asleep.

When Milton awoke the next morning, he discovered that his coach had been stolen.

All of his belongings had been packed in the coach, including most of his money—and the journal.

Milton alerted the innkeeper. The innkeeper interrogated the stable boy. The stable boy said that Mr. Crum had taken the coach out early. He didn't know why.

"Perhaps some emergency necessitated his leaving real suddenlike," suggested the innkeeper. "That must be it. Didn't have time to leave a note. Sure he'll return, squire. Sure of it."

When afternoon gave way to late afternoon and then dragged into dusk, the innkeeper had lost his confidence. He polished his countertop with increasing ferocity, as if with enough effort he could eradicate the stain not only on the counter but on the reputation of his safe, respectable inn as well.

Afternoon settled into dusk.

With an apologetic air, the innkeeper insisted Milton stay the night for free, and suggested (or rather entreated) that he wait until the next morning to call the police.

The next morning came. No coach. No Mr. Crum.

Finally they summoned the police. A mustachioed Constable asked a battery of questions, inspected this and that, and said that he would alert his men to be on the lookout for the coach, assuring Milton that they would do everything in their power to apprehend the criminal.

Days passed without word, and Milton paced by day and tossed and turned by night.

Milton blinked in the darkness as he lay in a strange bed in a strange room in a strange town on a night that seemed far too quiet, and his stomach soured, and his mind swam in fevers. In the shadow play on the ceiling he saw a shadowy Mr. Crum waving agreeably as he rode Milton's coach down an unmarked street in the town and vanished among the rookeries like the ball in a shell game.

He warned me. Thulemander warned me.

Muffled, distant, the crack of leathery wings.

The wings grew closer.

I'm trapped.

A titanic weight settled on the roof.

Go away.

The weight shifted. A stench of sulfur poisoned the air. He heard the town clock toll midnight. A year later, it tolled again, and a longer year until two, and it was past three on a night that would last a hundred suffocating years before Milton would curl up into a tiny ball again, and his fevers crumble into sleep.

The next morning he woke late, and loitered about the inn, waiting for the sun to evaporate last night's horrors, but it barely seeped through the overcast sky to drip in puddles here and there along the roadside, leaving the countryside mired in heaviness.

He ventured out, toward town.

"What do you plan to do, squire," asked the innkeeper, "regarding your travels and all?"

"I don't know," said Milton as he left.

He needed to walk. He needed to think.

An open road on empty country. Neither horse nor coach nor traveler afoot in any direction, as far as he could see.

His boots sloshed through wet grass, crunched gravel road.

The weather thickened. He muffled his scarf about him, dug his hands into his pockets, contemplated the road. He thought he heard feet walking in parallel beside him, but he refused to look.

"Say, did I ever tell you about Captain Tark?"

Thulemander fixed his eyes on Milton like a snake.

Milton ignored him, and kept walking.

"I didn't? Well then, surely you should know."

Milton clenched his fists in his pockets, and walked faster. Thulemander matched his stride.

"Captain Tark of the *Spinfire Charger*. Had quite a reputation among seafaring men in his day. Known throughout the world for his bravery. Only man to intimidate the Vikings into granting him safe passage through their waters. Used to harness sharks in Morecambe Bay and ride them like wild horses. A hardy man, even as sailors go, this Captain Tark.

"Well, he took it into his head to make a voyage west, beyond the Isle of Man, into waters that had never been charted. He believed he would find the fabled Mermaid Cove, where the mermaids decorated their coral cave with the treasures they salvaged from sunken ships. He was a man of great charisma, and he had earned the loyalty of his crew, so he convinced many of them that it was only three days beyond the Isle, and that the treasures they would find would make it all worth their while. They agreed to the voyage, and set sail.

"They sailed out beyond the Isle of Man. And you know what they found, Milton? Not mermaids. Oh, no! Oh, no indeed!"

Milton tried to evade his narrator, without success. He zigged and zagged, and Thulemander shadowed him.

"One morning they awoke to a curious sight: When they looked to the east, they saw the rising sun. But when they looked to the west, they saw a sky as black as night. Completely impenetrable. The sun rose higher, but had no effect on the wall of blackness. They were headed straight for it.

"Captain Tark refused to change course, even though his crew grew uneasy. They kept watching him as he sailed toward the black wall, expecting him to give the command to bring her full about. Ah, but by the time poor Captain Tark finally gave the order, it was too late.

"It was the sound that finally broke him. He heard the ocean pouring over World's End. It sounded like no other waterfall he had ever heard before, because he never heard the water hit bottom. It hissed over the Edge in a great mist, and disappeared. Tark gave his crew the order to turn, but by then they were much too close. The current had them, and

pulled them toward the Edge. His men set to the oars with all their strength.

"You know who paid them a visit then, Milton? Guess!"

Milton saw the wall of darkness before him, and he knew what was coming, but he did not say it aloud. "They heard wings. They smelled sulfur. They saw—"

"Go away!" blurted Milton. "I won't listen to you. I'm not going to fall over the Edge, so just leave me alone!"

Thulemander did not miss a beat. "There was nothing Tark could do to quell the panic that broke out. His men rowed until their oars cracked. Several grabbed their bows and began firing volleys at the great beast, but no arrow or dart could pierce its scales. It belched a great flame that ignited the sail. The bosun had begun sawing the lines to cut the sail loose, but he was too late: the mast had begun to burn. He leapt from the rigging straight into the sea. Four others mutinied and jumped ship in the lifeboat, but that was useless—they couldn't fight the current any better than the *Spinfire Charger*. They plummeted swiftly over the Edge. One man, when he ran out of arrows, broke open a barrel of biscuits and began hurling them at the Dragon, shouting insults and sobbing all the while. The First Mate howled commands into the bedlam while the men scampered about the deck in all directions like mad rats. He shouted himself hoarse, barking senseless orders and waving his arms. He had clearly gone mad. Another man drew his broadsword. Imagine! As if a broadsword might do him good!

"And Captain Tark? The Captain stayed steady at the helm. He steered an unswerving path straight toward World's End, straight toward the monster, until he tipped the *Spinfire Charger* right over the edge. The Captain went down with his ship, indeed—but it was not through any sense of duty: he had looked the Dragon in the eye, and the sight of it had transfixed him. He clung to the helm like a statue, even as he fell, *all the way down*."

A chilly silence.

Milton still refused to look at Thulemander. He tried to keep his voice steady as he said, very calmly, "Go away."

Thulemander drew up close to him, too close.

"Oh, my, aren't you brave! Steady as she goes, eh Milton?" There was amusement in his tone. "But Milton, where is your crew?" He wheeled in front of Milton now, who nonetheless kept walking, and he spread his hands as if to repeat the question. "A captain with no crew? That is very odd. Pray tell, Captain Milton, how do you expect to find your lovely Lorien with neither coach nor crew?"

Captain Milton marched on, mute. Thulemander's amusement wilted.

"You've lost your crew."

"Go away."

"You're lost," Thulemander hissed.

Milton stopped in his tracks and shut his eyes. He wanted to tear something to pieces. He wanted to scream, but he swallowed his scream, and it went down hard.

"If you don't have the courage to look at me when I speak to you, how will you find the courage to face World's End? What will you do when you encounter that wall of blackness?"

He didn't want to, but just to prove him wrong, Milton opened his eyes.

That was a mistake.

Because when he opened them, he looked into Thulemander's, and within them he saw the rigor mortis hand of Captain Tark fixed to the helm as he steered his ship into the abyss. He saw the men galloping off like nightmares in all directions while the mast splintered and rained down sparks and the rigging snaked down onto the deck and into the raging waves and the burning sail wraith-danced on the air like ash up a chimney flue, and the Dragon hovered above it all in the blackness, watching.

He closed his eyes again and clapped his hands over his ears, but he could not shut out Thulemander's voice. It tumbled through him like stones falling down a long dark well.

"When you fall over the Edge, Milton, you never hit bottom. There *is* no bottom. You just keep falling. You will grow *old,* falling. Are you that brave, Milton?"

He pinched his eyes tighter. Thulemander laughed. Milton clutched at the air, at nothing. Thulemander laughed louder.

He thought he heard the Dragon laughing then, but when he opened his eyes he saw no Dragon, and Thulemander was gone. A wolf howled somewhere in the distant forest, and the shadow-legions of dusk encroached on every border to steal away the countryside again. On the ground, he found a message scratched in the dirt in long, hooked letters:

Beyond This Point There Abide Dragons

Beyond which point? How close was it? Beyond that copse of trees, right over there? Was that it? Over that hillside to the north? Would the ground fall away right there? Which way? Which direction did Thulemander mean? He had drawn no compass rosette to tell him. He had only scratched his warning into the cold hard earth.

Milton froze. *Where would the world end?*

It could slope down into the shadows on the other side of the hill. It could decay into reedy marshes that oozed thick waters over the Edge. It could fragment into fjords or break up into craggy islands that floated in the Sea of Darkness, or the world could just end in a sheer-faced cliff that spilled down forever. Any of the walls of blackness that surrounded him now could be the one, the End, disguised as innocent night.

Somewhere, he heard the sound of the *Spinfire Charger* still falling. . . .

CHAPTER 14

A SECOND EXPEDITION LAUNCHED

A greasy little man knocked on the door of a perfectly symmetrical manor house situated in a perfectly manicured garden. A faded Toy Soldier answered and ushered him in. "I have an item here I think will interest you," he told the master of the estate. He handed over an unmarked, sun-bleached book. His host turned the pages delicately.

"You have heard of the recent discovery of Jonathan Larking's journal?" the visitor asked. "Well, I have discovered a second. Here it is, complete with information regarding the whereabouts of the cottage hideaway which houses his most spectacular work of art: the Lorien statue."

Adrian perused the book with increased interest.

"How did you come to find it?" he asked.

The flash faded from the greasy smile. "My sources are confidential. But I assure you, sir, the book is completely authentic. Completely, sir."

Adrian frowned at the book. After submitting it to the most thorough scrutiny, he opened his checkbook and withdrew his pen significantly.

"Your sum?" he asked.

The man's grin broadened.

The seller named his price. Adrian paid it, and the Larking journal was his. Within the week Adrian Plackett announced, assembled, and organized his own expedition team. He had not a moment to lose, what with the Crown Jewel of his Collection awaiting him in the Devonshire hills. No, sir.

His team made their preparations at the crack of dawn. In the coming and going and milling about they resembled bloodhounds preparing for the chase. Neighbors, street urchins, a reporter or two, and other wayside oglers watched the commotion as men packed things up and tied things down and helped the stable boy hitch up a team of restless horses to a coach equipped with every piece of gear an expedition might need. But most eyes watched Adrian, the leader of the hunt, as he oversaw everything in tight-lipped silence atop his fretting horse.

Only yesterday, he had stamped out another skirmish. This time the Dutch paintings in the upper gallery had rebelled. They had earthquake-tossed themselves all along the corridor, every one, and it had taken himself and two servants an hour to straighten them all. Absolutely infuriating.

Soon, order.

How long had he collected now? How long had he hunted? Years. And now he hovered on the verge of his final hunt. He would find this one statue and bring it back, and it would all be over. He'd be finished. His collection would be completed, perfect.

He gripped the reins, tight. His snowy gloves were stained with sweat.
His anxious team looked to him expectantly, wondering what was wrong.
He barked a command.
The bloodhounds leaped.
And the expedition was launched.

CHAPTER 15

UP THISTLE RIVER

On the wall of a music hall in Andover, a poster:

**Don't miss
THE DARING YOUNG DIVA
HEATHER GABRIELLE FEUR-DE-LYS
performing her controversial new repertoire of
experimental compositions by new composers
Twenty-two June,
Dirth and Brim's Company Theatre, Slackington**

Though he did not have the journal with him, Milton remembered every word. When he read the name on the poster, he heard Larking's voice chuckling in a summer that had been bottled up and shelved twenty years ago.

"Little Heather . . ."

Something bloomed inside Milton. The voice again:

"She is clearly a Feur-De-Lys. Song runs in her blood."

The something bloomed brighter: Hope.

Could it be?

He fished in his pocket for coins and found a few. He hired the first cab he found, and within the hour he was well on his way to Slackington to pay a visit to Dirth and Brim's Company Theatre.

For the first time since he left Radcliffe House, Milton began to settle a little and enjoy his journey. He stared out the window of the cab, watching the scenery roll by.

I'm going to Larking Land. Yes, I'm going to Larking Land.

Clop of hooves. Jingle of bridle. Scenes rolled by. A cottage. A row of haystacks. A farmer plowing his field.

Lorien, I'm on my way. I've found someone who can help me find you.

A tilted milestone. A yew tree, alone on an empty knoll. For an instant, he saw little Heather marching off through a copse of catmint to make her proclamations to a council of moss-bearded rocks.

(She'll remember the way. She must remember. How could anyone forget a place like that? Heather will remember, and she'll tell me and then I'll know where Lorien is, and I'll go there and find her, and then I'll be back in Larking Land with my friends. I'll run through the Oat Field with Braymouth and Lampyridae and we'll all find Lorien, and she'll bring the Book of Days, and we'll hike up Thistle River, all the way. . . .)

He recalled the one time he had traced Thistle River all the way to the source—or nearly so.

He had stepped through to the Oat Field, and it was empty. He did not see Braymouth, nor Lampyridae, nor any paper-lantern star resting on the horizon. He cupped his hands to his mouth, yelled to the plum-dark hills in all directions.

"Lorien! I'm home!"

And the hills shouted back in a smaller voice,

Home, home.

He scanned the crests of the far mountains, scanned the gray sky, half-wild with anticipation, but neither crags nor cloudbank gave away any secrets.

(Where is she on days like this? When I'm out here probing the countryside, where is she? Is she off tending to her work? Or is she watching me?)

"Lorien!"

Lorien, Lorien.

No other reply.

As always, Thistle River spilled down through the Oat Field in a million feather globes, threading down through the valley. He traced it with his eye, following it along as far as he could see.

She must be off rummaging through bluebell deeps, or towing a line of ducks somewhere, or something of that sort. Oh well, no matter. If she was busy, she would find him sooner or later, and if she was watching, she would answer at the right time (whatever that was). In either case, he saw no reason to delay his expedition upstream.

Capering up streamside, he began his jaunt. Every now and then, he glanced skyward, as if expecting rain. A single wren slung through the empty canvas, guided by its own internal map of migration, perhaps toward a vision of a warm nest which it could see, festooned in scrolls and swashes, a tremendous X held in the knobby grasp of an oak, ten, twenty, two hundred long quiet miles distant.

She would come soon enough. She always did.

Rain down to me, Lorien.

He walked up the familiar length that he had traveled dozens of times, measuring his progress by his passing certain oaks or pitches of slopes or twists in the river itself, but soon he reached unfamiliar territory. The familiar landmarks receded behind him, and now he had come farther up the river's course than he had ever been before. At first he could only think of what he might discover up ahead, but the more he walked, the more he became immersed in walking, and contented himself with the way the oats parted like an endless curtain with each swish of his step.

He reached a plateau where he could look off in any direction and see the Oat Field rippling along for miles.

How far did it go? Could he walk in any direction without reaching the end? Could he walk forever?

He began walking again, and his walk became an endless stream like the river itself that flowed beyond the counting of miles or days. He did not tire, nor thirst or give thought to food. He only walked and walked, and there were only oats rippling in all directions, very far and very close, and the sound of his constant step parting the stalks. Although the sun had never fully claimed the sky, it never set, even as the season began to turn into winter. The oats became thinner the farther he went, and finally thinned to mere windle straw that fell away to a hard crust of earth that crunched beneath his tread.

And he continued to walk.

Now on the trailing edge of winter, the oats made brave new beginnings: a new crop began to sprout, a thin blond forest warming the plain. Now he was a giant striding high above the glens and copses, taking them all in at a stride, straddling a hundred yards a stride, then twenty miles, then forty. His shadow eclipsed the wooded hamlets in its path. His shadow crossed over the villages, and boys reeled in their kites and raced each other home. Farmers hollered for their dogs, rabbits tucked themselves away deep in their warrens. Young daughters snatched dancing shirts off clotheslines and brought them in to mothers, who spun whirlpools in sparkling soups.

And on he walked through spring, into summer.

The oats grew taller and taller until they reached his shoulders, then kept on rising up to dwarf him in their wake, and now he found himself thimble-small in the basin of a tawny yellow forest, cooled by their shade from a brassy sun. He heard a crackling above him, like the murmur of pop-corn popping everywhere. The heat was swelling the oats, and the sound was the unfurling of their summer flags. He put his ear to a trunk. It was warm to the touch. The crackling reverberated through the grain, to its very core, as if it were a tall drum. He listened to a curious music trickling its rhythms through a rootwork that reached far, far underground.

And on he walked through summer.

He had arrived on the edge of autumn, and he could hear the storm-steeds rattling bridles in dark stables. What would he find next? Pumpkins swelling up as large as houses, and swelling larger even as he watched? Would the storm-steeds neigh and toss their silky manes, shivering lightning rods on bent and crooked barn-tops, and sending showers of nutmeg down on two hundred cups of warm milk in two hundred pie-warmed kitchens?

He began to think that he could just walk forever across the plain, and watch the ebb and flow of its rippling country, and just disappear into it all, weave himself into its rhythm. But just as he decided that the source of Thistle River didn't matter any more, he found it.

In the distance straight ahead, a windmill.

A tremendous windmill. A mountain.

The enormous vanes glided smooth and steady, almost hypnotically. As he drew closer, he heard only the faintest musical creak as they churned the air. They were so gently worn and weathered that they appeared fused into one, as though they had been whittled from a single block of wood.

Creak. Creak.

They glided so effortlessly, he thought that if they were standing still, he could set the whole colossal pinwheel in motion again with a tap of his finger.

He stopped to watch the vanes spin, and they looked so natural and right that it took Milton a moment to realize what he was seeing: no wind turned the windmill vanes. The windmill was *generating* the wind.

Then, what turned the windmill?

The ultimate source of Thistle River must lie inside.

The windows were shuttered tight. He heard no sound from within, no sound anywhere except the soft purr of the vanes.

At the base of the windmill, a door.

Not a door. An invitation. It said: *Come.*

Footprints leading to the door? None. If there had ever been, they would not have lasted long. Most of the ground was lost in the thick of stalks and straw and wandering weeds. Any footprints left would be swallowed up. A single path led to the door, but he found no trace of footprints, just a sprinkling of cinnamon.

On the door, a decorative cluster of corn and a brass knocker.

If he knocked, who would answer?

A Gingerbread Man, he imagined. He didn't know why. He envisioned a gingerbread host ushering him in with a nod that said, "We've been expecting you."

He didn't knock just yet.

Lorien, are you in there?

What if she wasn't? What if the windmill was empty?

What did it matter? He was as tall as a mountain, and thimble-small, and everything in between, and he could walk forever. If he chose, he could inflate himself with the warm air of Thistle River and balloon up like Lampyridae to sail over the crests and summits of Larking Land, and perhaps attract his own paper lamp to dog-lope on his heels.

Or, he could just fall back into the riverbed and count the fleecy stars bounding over him until he fell asleep. . . .

The river was fast and silky and endless in its rushing. He spread his arms windmill-wide, closed his eyes, and stepped in. The wind roared torrents of nonsense in his ears, flooded him with riptides of gibberish, and he gave in to that sweet sound, and already his clutter and cares were rinsing away downstream, rinsing away to nothing. The thistles scoured away every residue of worry, lightened him, sucked all his foolishness into its hissing tide and drowned it all away.

Rinse it all away.

When he opened his eyes, a galaxy swarmed over him. He drank in its galactic wind, and it rushed through him and scoured him through and through. He felt his fingers shriveling like bathtub prunes, and felt the stream coursing now through his veins like fireworks.

He tipped like giddy timber.

CHAPTER 16

THE IRON MAN

Nearly to Slackington now, Milton arrived in a small town outside Glastonbury late at night. He stopped at the first tavern he found, and tapped at the door. A servant admitted him, took his bags, and asked him to wait in the dining hall while he summoned the innkeeper, who could see to the business of furnishing him with a lodging and a hot cup of tea.

Milton entered the dining hall.

Sunken in a sofa opposite the fireplace, his back to Milton, sat a man.

Milton stopped short, studied him from a distance.

His hair was thick and unruly. He held a cup, but did not drink or move. He was so still that Milton would have sworn he was a creation of Madame Tussaud's, but when Milton noticed the tension in his neck muscles, and in the hand that clutched the cup, like vices clenched to their limit, he imagined the man might more likely be forged from iron.

There was no sound anywhere except the beating of Milton's own heart. He thought of retreating to wait in the hallway, when the servant returned to usher in another traveler who was also looking for a room. Glad at the sight of a chair and a moment's repose, the traveler took a seat near the Iron Man, kicked his feet up on a table near him, and attempted to start a conversation.

"Evening," said the traveler.

The Iron Man did not answer.

Too tired to take offense, and too relieved by delicious rest to let a hostile stranger spoil his good humor, the traveler turned his conversation toward Milton. He proved quite amiable, and soon put Milton so at ease with his idle talk that he felt safe in remaining with him in the dining hall, the Iron Man notwithstanding. Eventually Milton ventured to ask the traveler where in Slackington he might expect to find Dirth and Brim's Company Theatre. The traveler said he did not know, and in turn asked the Iron Man if *he* might be familiar with such a theatre and its whereabouts.

The Iron Man did not answer. He was staring into the fireplace, a hard, smoldering stare. But there was no fire.

The traveler asked his question again: Did he happen to know where they might find Dirth and Brim's Company Theatre?

"No," said the Iron Man coarsely. He took a swallow from his drink, and resumed his vigil.

Whatever the Iron Man saw so completely absorbed him that he was absent from their company. At this last retort even the traveler shrank back a little, finding more comfort in fetching some kindling than in chatting with their unsavory companion. He remarked to Milton how cold his ride from Cornwall had been, and began to build a fire.

"No fire," said the Iron Man softly. "Leave the fireplace alone."

"I beg your pardon, but I'm very cold," said the traveler, and continued to arrange the wood.

"Stay away from that fireplace!" the Iron Man commanded, very loudly this time. As he did so, he clenched his cup in his vice-grip fist so forcibly that he nearly shattered it. His bloodshot eyes never addressed the traveler. They only stared ruthlessly through him into the empty fireplace.

The traveler, surmising that his antagonist must be drunk, decided that it wasn't worth butting heads over a bundle of kindling. He opted to warm himself instead with a nip of toddy and a blanket in the comfort of his own room, far removed from the ill-tempered stranger.

The servant spoke to Milton under his breath: "Best to stay out of Mr. Hartshorne's way, sir. He's been in an evil temper. It's the brandy."

But somehow Milton sensed that the brandy did not entirely account for that hard, smoldering stare. The Iron Man saw something in that empty fireplace, and Milton saw its reflection in the face of the Iron Man. Something terrible.

CHAPTER 17

DIRTH AND BRIM'S COMPANY THEATRE

Every town has its outskirts, its riffraff, its rookeries, its frayed edges and dead ends. The curious thing about Slackington was that it seemed to consist of nothing but these. No matter how far Milton ventured into the town, no matter how many side streets he followed, he never found a main thoroughfare. No matter how many turns he took, he never hit a vein of foot traffic that suggested the wheels of commerce might churn steadily nearby. He found no landmark, no business quarter, no town clock, nor any other sign that might have indicated he had struck the center of things. The closest suggestion he did find was an old stone fountain at a crossroad, but the fountain had long since gone dry. Its giant grotesque fish pouted at the air, spraying nothing into a cracked and empty basin. Any coins that had rested beneath its waters had been snatched up, leaving only rusty rings; and the fish's eyes, too, bore heavy dark rings, painted there by a fine film of soot that blew in from the smokestacks that were everywhere in Slackington. The chimneys belched up opaque clouds that shipwrecked themselves on any building they might chance by, spilling their black cargoes down them in long streaks.

People? They came and went, blown in the newspaper tornadoes that skittered down blind alleys, or rattled by in the bellies of brittle coaches, bundled against the soot that dusted them, too, and painted dark rings beneath their eyes, like the fish. He walked briskly. Wrapped in his coat, his fists tucked into his pockets, he kept moving, looking. A muffin vendor barked at him. A street urchin ricocheted an old tin off a sagging wall. A knife grinder pressed a blade against his fire-spitting stone. Milton navigated his way through a thin tide of faceless pedestrians until side streets gave way to more side streets, these now empty except for a rare vagabond or stray dog. He remembered the street names the man in the pub had told him, and looked hard for them, though he really had no idea where he was.

A toothless man leered at him, sizing him up to guess the most effective way to beg a farthing, his eyes prying at him, especially his pockets.

Milton quickened his step.

Just keep walking, thought Milton, and he did. He dare not stop. Eyes peered everywhere, out of rubbish heaps and cracks in the walls.

What was the name of the street?

Down an alley. Down another. Front and center: a very large wall, plastered ten feet high with a circus-mélange of advertisements, all citing a familiar name: Dirth and Brim's Company Theatre. (A theatre of varieties.) Acts: Merismi the contortionist! Tyrolean stilt walkers! Trapeze acts! Madame Soufet and her dancing terriers! Plays: *Avarice* (a tragedy). *Terror's Lock and Key. The Trials of Mr. Witherspoon.* Shakespeare every Thursday! This week, *King Lear,* starring Alfred Durret in the leading role. On Fridays, sing along with Stewart. (He knows all the favorite ballads.)

The circus shouted. The circus roared.

Somewhere sandwiched between Merismi the contortionist and Madame Soufet and her dancing terriers, he found her:

THE DARING YOUNG DIVA

Dirth and Brim's Company Theatre presents the brilliant new soprano Heather Gabrielle Feur-De-Lys (daughter of the acclaimed lyric-soprano Isadora Napraxine Feur-De-Lys), who will give a public recital in a program entitled "Vocal Dare: Experimental Art Songs by New Composers." 22 June, 1871. Price of admission: *only 1s.* Doors open at 7:15.

Milton ran through a maze of alleys and side streets, chased by the cymbal-dazzle of the circus wall, until he found it: a Gothic theatre, tall as night.

A pair of muscular wrought-iron arms held two enormous gas lamps.

When he stepped closer, he could hear each lamp hissing, and smell the stench of its basilisk breath fuming the streets. Their heat cut through the oncoming chill of night, and attracted moths, which also settled on the Gothic wall in places. He looked up at the stone mass that vaulted through the vapors, and peering through that dark film he saw a row of carved faces peering back down. Below them, a sign:

DIRTH AND BRIM'S COMPANY THEATRE

The one and only.

What might be perched at the top of Dirth and Brim's, Milton could only guess, since the veil of dusk concealed its highest spire, but as he studied that opaque wall, he could not help but imagine that something was up there, watching him.

Peeling from the marquee, Heather's poster.

Behind the filigree grate at the ticket booth, no one.

At the theatre's entrance, an unnaturally tall, gaunt figure topped with a crooked top hat.

The figure noticed Milton, observed him a moment before beckoning:

"See the show, sir? You're just in time. Only one shilling."

Milton stepped closer.

The man reminded Milton of a rickety marionette. He was too tall and too thin to support himself by his own frame. Milton supposed there must have been a set of invisible strings holding him up. And in the same manner as marionettes, his entire person, unless some action demanded otherwise, entirely yielded to gravity. His shirt collar drooped. His coattails drooped. His shoulders drooped. His face was lost in that netherland between beard stubble and bare sallow skin, and fairly drooped, and his eyes were half-hidden by drooping lids.

"Are you sure I'm not early?" asked Milton.

"Not at all, sir. You are just in time. Right this way. One shilling, please."

Milton followed his usher through a dim lobby in which glinted the tapers of a few candles in a few mirrors. The gold giltwork glinted too, tracing a mere hint of an arch high above them. They traversed an expansive floor flourished with a riddle of mosaics in shades of marble, but from the shadows Milton could not read its design. Though his guide was not hunchbacked, Milton could still see the ridge of his backbone showing through his frock coat, further evidence that he was all frame and cloth. He moved, too, as though lifted along by an unseen puppeteer.

"Right this way, sir. Very nearly show time. Enjoy the show!"

With a slow and wavering gesture, the Puppet-Usher led him into the theatre proper.

Milton's heart raced as he stepped in.

The theatre was old and tired and filled with the echoes of a dozen Hamlets and two dozen Romeos. Cobwebs draped the balcony boxes in thin veils. Across the walls, a story of a forest deep had once been told, but now was interrupted by breaks in its narrative, since sections had either crumbled away or had been attacked by chisels. A fugue of trees rose bravely, but was chopped short. A towering trellis of elaborate vines laced up a column, but were pruned before they reached the top. At the apex of the proscenium above the stage, a hole gaped in the Gothic tableau like a missing tooth, suggesting that some august figure had once reigned over this palace from on high, but had since abdicated his throne. Even worse, the ceiling lacked a chandelier. Only a telltale hole in the ceiling design spoke of where one might have been.

Fugues. Dust. Visions.

The Puppet-Usher left him. Milton surveyed a sea of empty seats.

Two titans flanked the sides of the proscenium. At one time they labored to uphold tall pillars of something, but now whatever it was they had supported was missing. A centaur chased after nothing. An acrobat reached for an absent trapeze.

Organ pipes lined the two walls on either side of the stage, looming empires of Gothic steel.

Peanut shells. Orange peels. The smell of stale beer.

Milton dusted off a seat and tried to make himself comfortable.

Theatres, he had noticed, have a tendency to talk. With so many Hamlets and Romeos and other characters having fretted and bellowed and reflected their soliloquies off their golden walls, such buildings retain a perpetual echo that Milton, when he sat very still, could hear. He heard voices now, and in the dimness even saw the painted faces return in halos of limelight.

A Ghost spoke from the depths of a long dark well. His chains clinked a strange music when he moved.

* * *

Well Ghost: "Your face! I see it clear as the moon, reflected in the water. Of course, only a ghost can see another ghost. I see *you* there, my friend, poised on the threshold. What are you doing up there, amid all that clamor? Come and join me in this cool gray twilight. You don't belong up there. The twilight is your home."

Next, a Baroness, bedecked in ballroom gown and jewels, holding a mask before her eyes on a slender stick. She bent over Milton and studied him as though the mask were a magnifying glass.

The Baroness: "Oh my, what is this? A wallflower? An orphan? He looks so frail and delicate, like an eggshell. How did this poor, sickly creature stray in here? My, he looks anemic! Look at the way he flinches in the light! The poor thing's not fit to run around outdoors. Come here, child. What's your name? Can you speak? Something must be done for the poor boy. He needs care."

Another: the First Mate of an unknown ship. A dusky sail lapped behind him, and the deck creaked beneath his anxious feet.

The First Mate: "Sir, it has been over two weeks since we lost sight of land. We've no stars tonight, nor have we had any for the last four nights. I can't convince the others that you know where we are. They know we're lost." (Milton heard the toss of the tide.)

A fourth: a Fool, a cavorting cluster of diamonds all wild at the top with bells and a tall white grin.

The Fool: "Wuzza wuzza wuzza! Larking Land? Oh, yeah, brother! You *are* a Fool! That's so rich, I'm jealous I didn't think of it myself. Pray tell me, brother, what year was the wine you swigged up this fine tale from? I'll take a good pull on that bottle myself, and see what farce I can invent from its dregs. 'Larking Land.' Whooeee!"

Milton put up his guard, scanned the darkness, dug himself into his seat.

Well Ghost: "You are a foreigner up there. Haven't you always known that? Haven't you seen it in their faces, the bewildered looks people give you, as though they didn't know what to make of you?"

Baroness: "He's delicate, like a string of pearls. We must nurse him. Medicines! Call the doctor, and tell him to bring all his medicines! He'll need them all for this one, poor child."

First Mate: "I can't assure them unless you assure me. Tell me, Captain: Are we lost?"

The Fool: "Wait! I know who you are. You're Milton Radcliffe! Why, imagine that! The Master of Tomfoolery, here in our own theatre. I've heard all about you, brother. You have quite the reputation at the Cap-and-Bells Guild." (To the head atop his scepter—a miniature of his own head) "Aren't we in for a treat! Let's watch. It's our turn to be entertained tonight." (He sat backward in a chair in front of Milton, his legs flopping over the chairback. He and the scepter stared at Milton expectantly.)

Well Ghost: "I've haunted this well for one hundred and twenty-seven years. Know it by heart, like a nursery rhyme. Want a piece of advice from someone who knows? Walk your grounds. Learn them. Study them. Memorize them until you know every bump and furrow by name. Then, never leave them. You had begun good work in your Radcliffe House. Why abandon all that now, just as you were reaching your prime?"

Milton: "No, no. I'm not turning back. I'm going to sit right here and the show is going to start, and I'll see Heather, and then I'll meet her backstage after the show and tell her what's happened, and she'll take me to Larking Land. I know she will."

Baroness: "Castor oil! Mortimer's Tonic! Dr. Peabody's green elixir! A spoonful of each in the morning, two at noon, and three before you go to bed! Open wide!" (She pushed a spoon at him.)

First Mate: "Captain, if you have any reason to believe that this Land of Larking is within our reach, the men need to hear it—now. They're growing restless, and I can't placate them with sea chanteys and ale anymore. What do you have to say to them? Anything?"

Milton: "I won't fall over the Edge. I know where I'm going. Heather will take me there. I know she will."

The Fool: "Ha ha! 'Heather will take me there.' Ha ha ha ha!"

Well Ghost: "What if the journal is counterfeit? What if the pavilion is gone? What if it never was?"

Baroness: "We'll soak you in Epsom salts, and fish you out of the tub with a pair of tongs!"

First Mate: "If you don't know where we are, how much farther will you take us before you admit it, and turn us back? We have enough provisions to last us for the return—if we turn back now. Starting tomorrow, every day that we continue to sail in this direction means a day without food on the journey back."

The Fool (whispering to scepter): "Watch him! Watch him!"

Well Ghost: "What if Lorien is gone? What if the pavilion is in ruins? Do you really want to find out?"

Milton: "All of you, leave me alone!"

Baroness: "Listen to the way he breathes! He must be sensitive to spores in the air. He mustn't be running about in the filthy streets. I'll have the maid prepare a room for him, and clean it from head to toe."

First Mate: "First Mate's log. Forty days. Still no sight of the Captain's 'Land of Larking,' and we've left our own coast weeks behind. The men grow more restless every day."

Milton: "Leave me alone!"

The Fool (roars with laughter): "What beautiful deadpan. What timing. He's a natural." (To scepter) "Are you taking notes?"

Well Ghost: "A warm bed. A cup of tea, with two lumps of sugar. A walk down the familiar Tillington Road. That's your haunt, lad, so haunt it well. The job of a ghost is to guard his treasures. Don't you see what you're doing, lad? You're throwing yours away. I have all mine here, locked in this chest. And I've chained myself to it, see?" (He holds up his manacles demonstratively.) "My treasures will never leave me, and I'll never leave them."

Baroness: "A tub of salt water. A warm bed. A room with shutters to keep out the light. No spores to clog your delicate lungs. No harsh light to roast that anemic skin. It's a pity to be so sheltered, but we mustn't take any chances."

First Mate: "First Mate's log. Fifty days. Still no sight of land."

The Fool (roars again): "Look at that face! What a cad! Oh, brother!"

Well Ghost: "One hundred and twenty-seven years and not one heartbreak. Not one disappointment. Not one shattered hope. I have all my treasures here, locked in this chest. Here, let me show you. Here is my first kiss. You see? No one's touched it in all these years. I take it out and polish it and look at it every now and again, but I'll never surrender it. I'll never surrender it up."

Baroness: "Keep him out of the sunlight! The sunlight will roast him!"

First Mate: "First Mate's log. Over seventy-five days, and still no sight of land. Last night Briggs rushed down from the crow's nest to warn me. He told me he could hear the great waterfall of World's End. I told him he was delirious, ordered him to his quarters, and took the watch myself. I heard something, but I kept telling myself it was just the tide. . . ."

The Fool: "Stop! Stop! If I laugh any harder I'll split a seam! I concede! I'll turn in my cap and bells, unless you'll take me as your student. What do you say, brother?"

Milton: "No!"

Well Ghost: "Oh, isn't it beautiful? My first kiss, as fresh and new as the day it might have happened! Now what do you suppose would have happened had I popped it in my pocket and traipsed off into the world to find a place for it on some stranger's lips? Do you think I'm a fool?"

The Fool: "Wuzza wuzza wuzza!" (Waving his scepter in Milton's face) "I once knew a puny young runt, Who pursued an impossible hunt. . . ."

Well Ghost: "A day at the circus. I dreamed of starting a business once. Here it is! A pawnbroker. I'm a pawnbroker! Look! Look here!" (He holds up a photographic plate—blank.)

Baroness: "Now don't squirm and don't make faces, this is for your own good. Three spoonfuls. Open wide!"

First Mate: "We all know the legend. I can't stop them from telling tales. Last night Briggs filled the late hours with talk about all the ships that have gone over. They say once you fall, you fall forever, until all that's left of you is bones and ship's timber, falling for all time. My men don't show it, but they are ready to snap, I can tell. It's like watching a frayed line. After a while you just know when it's going to break." (The waters grew choppy. The sail whipped. The First Mate tottered.)

Milton : "I will *not* fall over the Edge! I know where I'm going. I'll be careful. . . ."

The Fool:

> "He tipped over World's End
> Where the Dragon-winds blend
> And that sure put an end to *his* stunt!"

Well Ghost: "Look here! I'm as rich as a king!" He added to the music of his chains the clinking of his treasures. He laughed and began to ripple away. For a moment his chains hung on the air where his arms had been, but they too quickly vanished.

Baroness: "I tried to help him, but he wouldn't take his medicine. Well, the orphanage has ways of dealing with such incorrigibles. Tut-tut. It's a sad thing. He seems to grow thinner by the minute. . . ."

She inspected her specimen under the scrutiny of her mask once again. The mask began to glow, and grew larger by slow degrees, until the Baroness disappeared behind it. Then the mask itself disappeared in a puff.

First Mate: "They won't follow you blindly any more, Captain. Give the order. Turn us back, while you still can." In a wash of the tide, ship and ship's mate dissolved away.

The Fool cackled, and the head on his scepter cackled in miniature. "Follow me, you fool!" he cried as he skipped in circles in the air, then cavorted, ran, and finally leaped over the edge of an invisible cliff, screaming as he trailed away like a shooting star into nothingness.

Milton clenched the arms of his chair, tight.

If I close my eyes, I can see Thistle River right now, threading through the hills. I can see it.

He did not open his eyes again until the show began.

* * *

From the abyss of the orchestra pit, the organ rose.

And seated at it, the organist, very smart in his evening attire, very matter-of-fact. His fingers worked the keys in neat methods, and following the score set before him, he brought various ranks of pipes to life. Evidently, some had slept for years, and now coughed and sputtered up their parts with wheezes and groans that nearly choked the music beyond recognition. But after the first few hideous measures while the pipes cleared their throats, they spoke up warm and loud. Throughout the prelude their voices improved, yet at certain intervals the organist would pull a few stops on the great panel before him to summon up a new rank, and the wheezes and groans would creep into the music again until the new members fell into tune. Although the music swelled as though accompanying some dramatic action, still the great crimson curtain had not lifted. The organ played to a faded velvet wall.

The prelude ended.

A new movement began.

The organist snatched at the stops.

He fired up one rank—dust riffled out, tracing the contours of the passage on the air in grim symmetry. Now he fired up the tallest rank—the floor tremored, and bands of rats scampered from their hiding places in blind panic, seeking refuge among the seats. Milton lifted his legs from the floor in horror. The organist stamped on a foot pedal—an earthquake shuddered through the floor and walls, rattling every loose seat and fixture. His feet stamped again to summon thunderbolts that raged a mad tune through the fugue framework that had risen up from other ranks, and now a voice as ancient as the Earth's deepest cave cleft the gloom with a tempest whose waves pounded in clockwork choreography a fury that would bring the stoutest sailor to his knees.

End of second movement. A new movement began.

By pulling various stops the organist transformed his instrument to one that spoke in a whole new tenor. First came fluted melodies, then reeds, harps, and bells, until the organ became its own makeshift orchestra, spouting up new polyphonies. Iron-clad towers snapped comet-tail flags, climbing higher and higher. Ebony horses tossed silky manes and overleaped tower and spire in relentless stampedes. Each hoofbeat branded the night with an amber print, the cumulative fury of galloping gridding out hot constellations which shifted and shunted to make way for new towers ascending ever higher toward a ceiling now miles lost in alabaster shadows and gold-stained gloom. Some grand design unfolded up there in the race of hoofbeats, but it was too vast and fierce to decipher, and disappeared all too quickly as the organist pulled again, transformed the music. The fury of his tempest subsided into ripples that ran with the rhythm of a brook, winding swift and smooth through the aisles, between the seats, and over the empty stage.

The curtain lifted.

And in a flash and a billow of smoke, Heather appeared.

The smoke rose. Her hands rose. Her voice rose.

And rose and rose and rose!

The song darted one way and now another, a deft bird who knew the contours of the night by heart and navigated them without effort. Though he could not understand the lyrics, Milton followed the melody wherever it took him. It came very close, nearly touched him, paused, mused, circled him, then corkscrewed up, up, higher toward the ceiling, and by the time he followed it there he discovered the chandelier above him was restored, sparkling like water. The elaborate vines, too, now climbed again all the way to the ceiling. The centaur chased a band of wood-nymphs, the acrobat found his trapeze waiting for him and turned flips in the air, and the burden of the titans was now restored. They supported a column of vases, each vessel itself titan-tall and overflowing with all manner of mysterious liquids: waters from the seven seas—green waters, and blue, and steel-gray, starfish-filled and cresting; resins of midnight, meteor puddles, the dregs of starry wines, moor fogs distilled to a luminous froth, summer lightnings wrung from dark summer clouds, and rainwater ricocheted off castle rooftops and amber spires. They all poured over the lips of the vases that stacked one atop another, splashing through the now-lavish giltwork in wild eddies, reaching all the way into the dizziness of the vaulted ceiling.

Heather sang.

Torches lit the palace more warmly now. Fern leaves towered, drooping feathered shade over the seats far below them. Grape clusters waxed on golden vines. Though he could not see it, Milton heard the brook trickling down through it all, adding its own melody to the music.

In a frieze high above the stage, a maid spun a stream of garlands from her spinning wheel which flashed and whirred to the tempo of the song. They blew about, tussled, landed all about the room in small flocks of marble, jade, and terracotta. They preened themselves, settled, draped along the balcony boxes in neat rows.

Heather sang.

In the upstage twilight, royal couples waltzed, revolving in dizzy turns, holding on to each other like children on a merry-go-round. From the echo chambers of a far balcony, a dozen princes rose, heavy with confessions. They loosed them in turns and fits into the listening night.

Ceiling revelry! Games overhead: Chariots cantered in a merry-go-round ring around the perimeter of the theatre's highest dome, towing laurel-crowned bronze men who chased each other without end. Coronation trumpeters raised flag-furled horns and bursted fanfares counterpoint to the organ. Horses leaped over hurdles. Harlequins ratcheted around maypoles.

A glass staircase, solid but translucent, spiraled straight up through the festivities and on upward through a hole in the vaulted dome, through which Milton could make out the merest hint of a cotton sky. He rose from his seat to climb the staircase, but before it solidified completely, it dissolved away. Although the organ still played, Heather's voice had trailed off, and all the splendor it had evoked wavered, fluxed, faded into a mist, and finally burned off in the heat of the footlights, leaving Milton once again amid dust and gloom.

The organ stopped.

The curtain fell.

The performance had ended.

Milton closed his eyes in the hope that when he opened them, he might find the palace that had shimmered away. But desolation had returned.

He looked about him, saw no one. Both organ and organist had disappeared as mysteriously as the palatial surroundings, leaving the theatre empty. Still, Milton cast several furtive glances about before he approached the proscenium, touched a foot upon the stair that led backstage, then froze.

A cold poured through him like lead.

How could he go up?

On the other hand, how could he stay? How could he leave?

One by one, the footlights extinguished. The theatre was plunged into deep shadow. Milton waited for his eyes to adjust to the dark, but it proved nearly impenetrable. He could make out little more than the outline of the stairs immediately before him. He tried to turn back, but couldn't. When he tried to calm himself by closing his eyes again, he could still see the afterimage of the palace, rippling away into nothing.

"Lorien?" the name trembled on his lips.

Could he see a single firefly? a smoke ring? a solitary moth, sparking the night?

Nowhere.

If I don't move now, I'll lose all that. I'll lose it all. I'll never see her again. I'll never see any of them.

He drew a deep breath.

Noticing a guttering lantern, he picked it up and nursed the flame to a dim glow, then held the lamp out, its panes rattling in his unsteady grip, and probed a gloom too thick to yield up all its secrets. It gave up only fragments: A shadow-crate. A curtain-phantom. A Grecian fountain gone dry. Fireworks left over from a gala night that never happened, left to molder. The smell of gunpowder. Or . . .

Brimstone?

He took another deep breath, drew it in so deep that everything inside him that threatened to fly apart or fray into shreds was, for an instant, stilled. He steadied the lantern, collected himself.

Thulemander whispered something into Milton's ear that he could not make out.

He climbed the first stair.

Somewhere off in the darkness, Thulemander continued a recitation that Milton now recognized: He was quoting the passage from *Cosmographie* which described the Sea of Darkness.

Milton ignored him, and stepped blindly into the blackness backstage.

CHAPTER 18

TOWARD THE
SEA OF DARKNESS

Greasepaint. Ropes. Damp play-bills.

Where Milton at first felt paper beneath his feet he now felt the rustle of leaves, and where at first he saw old curtains and ripped scenery flats bat-flapping above him, he now saw a thick forest canopy, broken in places to reveal a night sky. Nailed to a dead tree trunk, a sign:

Beyond This Point There Abide Dragons

Beyond the sign, the forest thickened. Soon the treetops blocked out the sky entirely. Milton slogged his way through mulch and twigs. He wove through rootwork and branches that encroached on each other in tangled knots, and through thick meshes of thorns in a forest that was far too quiet, vast, and vacant. Some trees were freckled with a fungus that looked like tar. Others were twisted into grotesque forms quite unlike trees. He knocked on the trunk of one tree with a curious bark. It was petrified.

He felt a dampness seep into him. The wind shook dead twigs loose which filtered through the branches both near and far, and the sound of them, along with the echoes of his own rustle and crunch through the brambles, gave him an idea of how immense the forest was. He guessed that it rambled on for mile after petrified mile, and it all looked the same no matter which way he headed. He had no idea where among it all he might find Heather.

A voice smoldered up from nowhere like a dream, languished, faded away.

Which direction did it come from? Milton couldn't tell.

He tried to walk softly, partly to listen for the voice, and partly for fear of being heard (by what, he did not know), but mostly because the sound of his steps reminded him how huge and forsaken the whole place was. The silence became unbearable, and his lone footsteps breaking it only made it worse. The deeper he went, the more he began to notice little signs that told the story of how this forest had become uninhabited.

See those empty nests? A hundred crows tossed in brimstone squall by the stroke of a single spiteful wing. That owl feather underfoot? Pinwheeled off course in a poisoned hurricane. A delirium had boiled in hares' blood and sent them scampering hot to the deepest holes in the deepest warrens, never to surface again. The wolves had sipped the water downstream of the great black-adder tongue that had sipped there first and tainted the river. Those who drank foamed at the mouth and fell to the ground in fits. Those who didn't, fled. Milton could see it written piecemeal all around him: the pockmarks of mad boar tusks drilled into tree trunks. Stampedes of wild-eyed elk terror-trampled paths through the brambles, all running away from the direction he was heading. . . .

He marched onward.

Nothing lived here. All the inhabitants had been flushed out in a mass exodus. A Conqueror had risen up from the far abyss and driven them out.

He saw a green glow to one side of him up ahead, and heard the voice again. Although he still could not be certain where the sound came from, he imagined it was from that same direction, so he veered that way, craning his lantern high. He found a different growth of forest there whose branches were draped with a green lichen that hung down in long, spindly beards. The trees themselves were less dense here, and formed a rough corridor through which Milton made his way. When the voice died out again, he froze for just an instant and listened hard. When he heard only his own breathing and the rattle of the lantern pane in his unsteady hand, he resumed walking. Surely he would find the source of the voice at the corridor's end?

He marched onward.

Up there, in the tree boughs up ahead, what was that? A glint of metal? He slowed his pace and raised his lantern higher to puzzle out what it was before venturing too close, but he couldn't make it out from a distance. With great caution he drew closer, and to his horror he realized what was strung up in the trees. They were suits of armor, blackened like tin cans roasted in a furnace, cooled into rigor mortis gestures and hoisted to their perches. Dozens lined the corridor on both sides. Some of them were very old, and streaked and rusted from many soft rains. Some were dismembered. All were battered. In each he could read the history of their demise. This one fell from a great height. That one was pierced through the breastplate. This one had lost a gauntlet, another had lost much more, and that one was flattened nearly beyond recognition. A few of them were headless.

Below them, shields had been tossed for scrap. They stood like tombstones in the mulch. Milton tried to read the coats of arms to see if he could discover any famous knights fallen here, but that proved futile, since all shields were scorched beyond recognition.

Had the Dragon hung them there? It might have strung the little beetle-men up as trophies for its own amusement, but that hardly seemed likely. Who had done it, then? Did some other creature stalk these woods?

Or had Thulemander done it?

Thulemander, yes, as a final warning for those who didn't heed his signs. Milton could see him at the top of a ladder hammering away, at once posting a warning too stern to ignore and also taking out his vengeance on those who hadn't heeded him. *What did I tell you? You didn't listen, did you? Fool.*

The dampness of the forest penetrated Milton to his very bones. Shivering, he set down his lantern on a blackened shield, and wondered how he could have become so lost on a journey that had seemed so simple, so essential. There was no use calling out to Braymouth or Lampyridae or to anyone. He had crossed Thulemander's threshold, and anyone who might have heard his buried cry from a thousand miles off would presume him beyond help. Which gave rise to another chilling thought: If he just sat down there and never stood up again, who would notice?

Lorien would, somewhere.

She would notice because of the Book of Days.

The longer he spent away from Larking Land, the larger the book grew. He imagined that, in the same way that he had built his secret room to guard the painting portal, Lorien preserved his Book of Days in some similar keep, where all the caramel photographs appeared to illustrate its pages. But a book can only grow so large. What would happen to all the days that wouldn't fit? As he stayed away for weeks, then months, then seasons and years, where would those lost days go? What would happen to them? Lorien might notice that the book had stopped growing and wonder what was keeping him away. She might be sitting before the book now. She might be floating out the window to speed over the golden hills in search of him, but she would not find him.

Book of Days, wait for me.

Searching the screen of branches overhead, Milton found a single hole through which he could glimpse the night sky. He spied one watery star, crisp on a night so clear and cold, yet shimmering and nearly winking out, as if sinking away into a night of another time. It struck him that he was like the star, that he didn't belong in this place, and that his own deliverance from it lay now in his hands, unspeakably fragile.

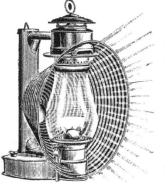

His lantern flashed weakly. By accident, he caught the star's reflection in a suit of armor still fresh enough to throw a little light back. He could not understand why this grim mirror fascinated him, but he studied the point of light that swam there, firefly-bright.

It was strangely beautiful.

The voice returned.

High, gentle, pure. It floated above the forest somewhere, or beyond, yet sounded closer now than it had before—but perhaps that was only a trick of one solitary echo straying through ravines. Something about the sound told him the singer knew him through and through, and was now calling up everything within him to stand up, gather his courage, and find his way out.

When he stood, he was shaking.

It was a voice too beautiful to belong in such a place, and he didn't understand what had brought it here. It must have traveled very far, originated from some distant place that was safe from this forsaken rim of the world. In a forest where nothing lived, it lived, and it brought with it desire and hopes long laid to rest but now found again and burnished and renewed. Where was its home? It might come from any place but here, not here, and he was glad such a voice could trip lightly through this shadow without stain. He drank in its weightlessness, and tasted a sweet air there filled with promises made and kept, and now holding out one more promise to him now, a pearl, a gift: *Keep walking. I am here, waiting.*

The dampness of the forest had seeped into his bones. He picked those bones up, and marched onward.

The voice trailed away to nothing.

Something eclipsed the star.

Only for a moment. It reappeared almost instantly. Nevertheless, Milton could not deny what he saw, nor could he ignore what it meant. Some immense body had flown overhead.

It's come for me, he thought. *The Conqueror.*

Is it reading my mind right now? Even from way up there, can it sift through my thoughts? Does it know how scared I am? And does fear whet its appetite?

He knew the answer: With each breath it drew in the flavor of panic named Milton Radcliffe, boiled the sump of lava gases in its air-balloon belly, anticipating not the morsel, but the long draught of terror that would come before it ever descended. Did it dine on that? Maybe that's why it had drawn out this cat-and-mouse game over so many years. It snacked on his dread. Maybe it would never strike. Maybe it would chase him all his life, savoring his cold sweats and fever dreams while Milton slowly decayed into madness, and then wouldn't he too be a creature of chaos? Wouldn't he have joined its ranks?

Somewhere high in the night a mammoth bat wing flapped a hot wind down through the forest, down through the corridor of trees. It stirred the armor like wind chimes. The metal a rusty chorus: *Go back, go back, to your warm snug hole, all rosewood sleeping and teacup settled, and never come out here again.*

Radcliffe House seemed a hundred years back, lost.

He stole away from the knights before they could murmur more warnings.

The crunch of his step was far too loud. *Shh. Softly. It'll hear.*

Through gnarled vines that choked out trunks, through lichen curtain and moldy sinkholes, he made his way to the forest's rim. Beyond it lay a moor all waste and blood-red earth, and scattered bones. The ground was blistered and scorched in places where skyborne fireballs had blasted down toward figures begging mercy, or shaking fists in defiance, or running with all their strength. Snapped lances were strewn like matchsticks. And one long impossible sprint away, he saw a single door. Just a door, with neither frame nor wall around it.

I must reach that door, thought Milton.

A stench of brimstone.

If I stay in the forest, I'm safe. It can't find me in here.

But how long could he stay?

It's waiting for me to come out and run for the door. I know it.

How do you tell whether or not a Dragon is stalking you? It does not roar down in a thunder. It does not gape and bellow. It is too smart for that, too artful.

It circled far, far overhead. Its nostrils flexed, and its tongue flickered the air, tasting the aroma of fear that sweated through Milton's pores. It listened for his racing heartbeat deep beneath the leafy canopy where he was hidden, and it drank all his fevered thoughts. It sifted through them, found his plan, rolled it under its hot mottled tongue, savored its sweetness, and waited.

Milton crept along the edge of the forest, eyeing the door.

Heather Gabrielle Feur-De-Lys

A mile above him, a yellow eye kept a patient vigil on the little rabbit-man scuttling through the damp and dank of a decaying forest.

All at once, Milton was hot and cold and chilled and racked and broken through with fevers, and every hair on his body prickled. He took in deep breaths, huffed them out in vapors. He took one hard long look at his target, the door that was impossibly far away, and braced himself for the run.

It would take him some time to circle around again.

Maybe it can smell me, or smell my fear, and maybe it can read my thoughts, but not everything, it can't know everything every minute. If I cloud my own mind and just think of nothing, and not let it know when I'm going to run. . . .

He did not think. He did not plot. He did not blink.

He ran.

He ran fast and hard and true and the heartbeat hammering in his ears told him that he was alive, and that no ancient monster would swallow up the night with him in it, not so long as he could run this powerfully and arrow-straight fueled by a fire burning in his own lungs. Each stride pushed him harder and faster through the blood-red night toward the single door.

Two vast prehistoric sails spread out over half a mile of darkness, trimmed and turned an armored leviathan deftly in the air, and gently descended.

A crack of wings, a rush of seething air.

Run!

A jet of flame shot down and scorched the earth in front of him. Milton reeled, cried out in terror, galloped madly in another direction on rubber knees and feet that did not think of stopping but only hurled him toward a white-hot spot that burned in the center of his vision long after the fireball had withered to a mere wraith. The moor spun at a tilted pitch, settled, slowed to a halt long before his vision came back into focus on a door now rippling behind a curtain of heat waves. Cinders rained from the sky.

You missed! You missed me!

Even so, he sprinted, and reached the door.

The name on the door: HEATHER GABRIELLE FEUR-DE-LYS.

He swung the door wide.

CHAPTER 19

HEATHER

She screamed.

Milton flattened himself against the door.

She screamed again.

A piano. A bare wooden floor. A tall, splendid mirror.

And Heather Gabrielle Feur-De-Lys screaming.

She was a banshee, clawing at the air with her hands and pulling down bats and furies and phantoms and fiends and a menagerie of unseen beasts that flocked about her. Her voice rose and fell like a gale. She writhed, swayed, swooned, then crouched, then sprang, then whirled like a cyclone, then loosed a cry that surely chased beasts, bats, and phantoms scampering back into their damp havens to cower and shudder.

When her cries subsided she caught a glimpse of herself in the mirror, and stopped a moment to study her face. She held her hands up to her jaw, smoothed it, dropped it wide open, wagged her head and let her chin wag loose while she massaged her cheeks. She had seemed to settle down, at least for the moment. Then she turned to the piano.

She pounded on it. First with the flat palms of her hands, then with cat-claws, then two-fisted in mad volleys on the keyboard, crashing down avalanches of noise. The high notes ricocheted off the walls and ceiling, the low notes shook Milton's very frame, and her voice, matching each landfall with shouts first low and round, then bright and shrill, trumpeted through it all in percussive blasts.

Her tantrum now subsided to a reckless, luxurious fretting to and fro, wherein she lolled her head and moaned lamentably, and sketched the contours of those laments on the air with her hands. She hardly paused to breathe between the moans, which were by turns harsh and twisted, or soft and smoky, or long and deep and drenched in longing. At the end of a particularly extravagant groan which trailed off into coarse gravel nearly as soft as a whisper, she stopped, raised her head, and looked at Milton.

He opened his mouth, but nothing came out.

Heather was in the fits of a rehearsal when she was interrupted by a timid little mouse. He clutched his hat so tightly between his hands that he nearly crumpled it, and kept fidgeting from one foot to the other. He didn't seem to know what to say.

"May I help you?" asked Heather.

"Excuse me," squeaked her visitor.

She waited patiently. The mouse's eyes darted evasively.

"I just wanted to tell you how much I enjoyed your performance this evening," he said to his shoes.

"Oh, thank you very much!" She smiled.

"It was . . . It was the most beautiful performance I've ever heard."

"Oh my, thank you!" She might have blushed, but her histrionics had already filled her complexion with a ruby glow.

Again the mouse appeared to be at a loss for words. He was wringing his hat now.

"Well, I hope you'll be able to attend my next concert." Heather nodded agreeably, and turned back toward the piano.

"Do you give many recitals?" he stammered.

"Yes. In London, mostly. And Paris. Well, I'm very glad you enjoyed it. Now I must get back to my rehearsal, but it was very nice to have met you." She raised her hands in menacing fashion above the keyboard.

"Wait! Um . . . excuse me again," said the visitor. "I'm sorry to interrupt you, but if I may have just a few minutes of your time, I'd like to ask you some questions, if I may."

He presented his card. He introduced himself. He explained about his search for the works of Jonathan Larking and the recent discovery of Larking's journal, about his attempt to recover the works in the secret cottage that Larking referred to as the summer pavilion, and about the recent betrayal of Mr. Crum. She was immediately absorbed in his tale. When he first mentioned Larking's name, she lit up like a candle, but did not interrupt his narrative. He interrupted it himself when he reached a juncture that he didn't know how to breach. He stopped and started a few times, and began stammering again.

"It's funny. He mentioned a little girl who had hidden in his coach and stayed in the pavilion with him for a whole summer. Evidently, this is the only person other than his wife who ever visited there. The little girl was the daughter of a friend of his, a singer—"

Unmistakably, a blush. And a laugh.

"I do think it's time I took a break. Would you care for some tea, Mr. Radcliffe? I'm very interested to hear more about this journal."

"Any details you recall that might help me find the pavilion, anything at all, would be enormously appreciated." Milton had pleaded a dozen different ways before he had finished his first cup of Earl Grey.

Heather remembered what she could, relating it all with great detail, but it soon became clear to her that Milton had a very poor sense of geography. He recognized not a single place that she could name. Not only was he unfamiliar with the major roads, towns, and landmarks of the region, he also had a curious propensity for mixing all her directions up, even as she gave them. After repeated attempts to convey to him the most basic itinerary, she resorted to the desperate measure of tracing paths with her finger on the table. She even enlisted plates and cutlery to further illustrate her points. But Milton was baffled.

After numerous reiterations on Heather's part, and after much concentrated study, Milton finally convinced himself that he understood her directions. When she asked if he intended to continue the journey without hiring any assistants and without a guide, he said he felt confident he could find his way on his own. But he turned a shade paler at the question. Heather asked if he would not like written instructions?

No, no, that wasn't necessary.

He studied the arrangement on the tabletop, nearly sweating.

Heather produced a sheet of paper and drew a map.

Somewhat embarrassed, Milton took it.

Heather changed the subject, finally offering an explanation for her rather unorthodox method of rehearsal, a technique designed to liberate the voice, which she called VOCAL DARE.

VOCAL DARE, a technique taught to her by her mother, was a method of freeing the voice by first freeing the singer of inhibitions. A singer, Isadora used to say, must be willing to hear herself make all kinds of sounds without cringing or holding back. The uninhibited tone, she said, came from the uninhibited singer. Believing this philosophy as firmly as she did, it naturally followed that she instructed Heather not only to sing scales in the normal *do, re, mi* fashion, but to sing laughing scales, sliding scales, topsy-turvy scales that sluiced up and down and banked and curved as they went. Then came lessons in barking and cooing and whooping like a crane and neighing like a horse and honking like a goose and hooting like a great barn owl, and even croaking like a frog; and after that came lessons in growling and strutting and clawing the air as a lioness might, and banging out rhythms on the piano top in a great oxen stampede. Finally, Isadora would gallop around the studio waving her arms in great alarms and shouting, "Fire!" in every kind of voice imaginable, then heaving imaginary buckets of water in every direction with all her might, or else pirouetting like a cyclone and raising up a wail to a piercing pitch.

Great fun, this VOCAL DARE, and eminently practical. It really did work wonders, Heather declared.

Milton said he imagined it did.

He seemed to be waiting for something, though Heather couldn't tell what. In the little ebbs of silence in their conversation, she sensed a hopeful expectation from him, as though he were thinking of a wish he had made that any minute might come true. Without knowing what it was, she could neither help it along nor offer solace if it failed to appear, so she appeased him by following attentively as their talk dwindled to mere trifles and pleasantries. By the end of it, when Milton thanked her and bade her good night, she sensed that the wish had not come true. She could hear it in his voice.

"Good night," she replied, not knowing what else to say.

With a bow and a final word of thanks, Milton left to resume his expedition.

What a curious man, thought Heather.

A minute later, he returned.

He treadled his hat in his hands nervously, as though he had something to say but couldn't bring himself to say it. Only when Heather threw a question mark up in the air with the arch of an eyebrow did he shuffle back to her table, blooming crimson.

"I forgot—"

She held up the map. The sight of it deepened his crimson all the more. Heather tried to smile the right sort of smile, a kind smile, a smile that didn't laugh. Buttressing his dignity with a formal air, Milton stumbled through a reiteration of thank yous and farewells, bowed on his way out, and with a snap of the door, vanished.

The next day, Heather returned to the theatre.

She lounged in a chair and leafed through her stack of sheet music. She had started off looking for a song, then forgot what she was looking for and merely leafed through the sheaf of notes without seeing them. What did she see instead?

A mouse-man chasing after a marble woman. A mouse-man who talks to his shoes.

Most curious.

As she leafed further through, she found amid the yellowed pages an article about a place she had visited a very long time ago, a forgotten cottage from a forgotten summer, stuck there like a bookmark, waiting for her. She traced her finger over the newspaper clipping ponderously as she read it again:

> . . . the discovery of Mr. Larking's private journal has revealed the existence of a secret cottage wherein the painter retreated for the summer months to create what he considered his greatest works. . . .

That summer *was* a masterpiece.

Was the Bluebell Forest still standing? she wondered. A forest. Yes.

How long ago it seemed, and yet . . . it was almost as though a piece of it was always with her. Sometimes the glare of the footlights would dazzle her, so when she walked backstage, the sudden plunge into darkness left her half-blind. When she closed her eyes and waited for her vision to recuperate, she would see the briefest trace of fireflies sparking the evening air. Open them, and the theatre would return, the fireflies fade.

Voices are strange things. They come and they go. A voice might go with a cold, or from a long time spent away from practice, or from lack of exercise, or—

Lack of bluebells? Ridiculous!

No. Not ridiculous. Absolute fact.

Oh, *that summer!*

She could almost taste it. She could almost feel her voice returning to her already.

Heather could not point to the morning she woke up to discover her voice had left her. She had lost it somewhere between Paris and London. Or London and Paris. Or perhaps in Vienna. Or perhaps somewhere between the pavilion summer of twenty long looking-glass years ago and the torrent of days that had all run into each other since then. Now, each day was not quite done before the next began, with one show after the other and a mad rush of top hats and whirling capes and an avalanche of calling cards and bouquets and receptions and banquets and troops of freshly ironed critics adjusting their eyeglasses like microscopes and then all the long wild rehearsals sandwiched in between. Everything rushed together in a crescendo that left her dizzy.

Did Milton Radcliffe have any idea how close he was? Did he realize he was no more than a day away?

Of course not. The thought of him bumbling into the countryside without a guide made her wince. The mouse would never find his way home.

On the back of his card, he had written the name of the inn at which he was staying. She examined the address, written in minuscule cursive. The letters were slightly shaky, hesitant.

He'll never find it alone. It's so cleverly tucked away.

She found the song she had been looking for, and began to rehearse. Anyone who listened might have done either of two things: they might either have melted in awe, or else called the police. Of course, she didn't care which, and in fact didn't care what anyone thought of her vocal exercises. She sighed her descending sighs until she ran out of them, then fell silent.

She ended her rehearsal early, and took a walk. The street looked worn, tired. She came back early.

I never did take that holiday. I need it. It's time.

As soon as she returned, she began packing.

After she finished gathering her belongings, she jotted a quick note to Philippe and left it conspicuously on her desk.

> *Dear Philippe:*
>
> *Decided to take my holiday immediately. I suspect I shall find my voice somewhere in the hills of Devonshire, so off I go. I'm afraid I must rush off this morning and I know how you loathe being awoken early, so I didn't wake you. But rest assured I travel with good company. Will explain all when I return. Will meet you in London in a fortnight or so.*
>
> *Best wishes,*
> *Heather.*

And off she went.

When she had first told Philippe that she had lost her voice, they both agreed a holiday would be just the thing to find it. The question was, where?

Where had she lost it? And how?

Philippe had known better than to ask.

She had left her voice somewhere between the clamoring Slackington street where her coach jostled along right now, and the pavilion of twenty years ago in a summer that sat silently in memory, but would not quit. It still burned brighter than any spotlight, and hotter. Her voice was waiting somewhere in that long tumultuous stretch.

She would find it, she knew, in the Forest of the Bluebells.

CHAPTER 20

QUEEN OF THE BLUEBELLS

Her brougham rambled down a long rural road that wound this way and that before it found the little inn (which resembled, as closely as any inn could, a little mouse-hole). Inside, the little mouse-man sat before a tall window, absorbed by the view.

Milton could not have known that she would come, yet some uncanny sense told her that he had been sitting there ever since he had left the theatre, waiting for her. She didn't know *how* she knew it—perhaps it was something in the way he was looking out the window. There was a deep patience in that looking, the kind that comes from years of waiting. He was so steeped in his searching of the blank sky that he had hardly noticed her when she entered the inn. Only when she spoke his name did the word break his reverie the way a pebble sends ripples through a pond. So too did the word send him up on his feet, fumbling and stammering, and blurting out greetings mixed up in an avalanche of thanks.

Her same uncanny sense told Heather that if she *hadn't* appeared, still he would have waited there by the window—for days, months, years, with no plan in his head but all the patience in the world, and a fascination with that empty sky which held some promise for him that she could not fathom.

She told him of her intention to visit the pavilion herself. She thought that if he wanted a little company, they might travel there together. Might she join him?

Milton bowed in agreement. A marvelous plan.

Excellent. Well, it was time for her walk. Would Milton care to come along?

Could Milton possibly have blushed a brighter shade of red? Could he possibly have bungled the answer "yes" more thoroughly than he did? Despite his affirmation, she thought by the looks of him that at any minute he would dart back to his room, wedge himself within the hole of a Swiss cheese round, and refuse to come out. But he didn't. He followed her outside.

Behind the inn there was a garden, and beyond it, a little stretch of wild grasses woven through with walking paths.

"The perfect place," said Heather.

They walked.

They hadn't walked far before Heather noticed that Milton began to look about him as though he didn't know where they were. An expression of alarm briefly crossed his face, but passed as he mirrored her footsteps and listened to her idle talk about singing and travel and paintings. When she spoke of Paris, he listened with the awe of a child absorbing a fable. When she spoke of paintings, he lit up like a boy in a sweetshop. When she asked him anything about himself, he became very interested in his shoes, and didn't know what to say, really.

She decided to let questions rest awhile, and in the space of that silence, Milton trembled on the edge of a question of his own. Finally, after much hesitance, he asked it: What was it like, this pavilion?

Heather described a typical day from that summer that had been anything but typical.

She had awoken in the kiss of sunlight, arrayed in linen-deep sleep, and shrugged off her blankets of hibernation. Cat stretch. Dog yawn. Nimble bounce up into dawn brass spilling through cumulus curtain. Song-skip to table for morning feast. Milk tide flooding the oat hills. Raisin gems winking in the tide. Spooning up great mountains and sliding them down with slurps and sloshes.

Soon, the bluebells.

Morning coronation. Don the royal robes. Procession to the hillside where she took up her reed-scepter, balanced her minty crown upon her bounteous curls, and high-stepped down the switchback first, then through thicket curtain to her Queendom, where her subjects awaited her.

"Queen Feur-De-Lys!" they shouted. "Queen of the Bluebells!"

A regal saunter. A stately nod.

"Queen Feur-De-Lys! Queen of Ants and Beetles and Moths! All hail!"

A refined carriage of the chin. The scepter rose and fell with every step.

"Queen Feur-De-Lys, come christen me!"

A fanfare of wrens. A ruffle and flourish on the beetle-shell drum as the stout-armored insects cut a path before her, announcing the Coming of the Queen. The barley stalks unfurled their tapered flags, and a confetti of yarrows dotted her path.

She glided sedan-chair-smooth through tall blue ranks to dub those who came and knelt before her, according to their deeds. She called each one by name (for naturally, she knew them all), and raised them to their title. Arise, Sir Fefferidge Foxglove, tailor to foxes! Arise, Sir Tartantus, Duke of Ants! Arise, Sir Snigbricklet Beetle-Man! Arise, Sir Bofflepodmoffle Potato Bug!

Pollen rain. Wren flurry. She seated herself upon her bluebell throne. Nellerelium landed atop her scepter fanning multicolored wings to cool them from his long flight.

"Nellerelium, I command you: tell me what you saw!" said the Queen.

And the butterfly told.

The Flight of Nellerelium

I ventured from my roofbeam nook in Barn,
The sunken hall of moth and mouse.
I trimmed my wings to touch the walnut wind
That rushes toward your noble House.

Past rusted lantern, ivy-tangled fence,
Past capsized plow and moss-drowned wall,
I funneled through a cyclone's eye, adrift,
Then skipped through storm and thistle-squall.

I saw the cricket orchestra disband.
They tiptoed through the tawny weeds,
Their slender cellos boxed, their oboes hushed,
The warm light softening their reeds.

They left a spate of nocturne notes behind,
The ground wild-scrawled by grassy plumes,
But dawn's gray touch was simmering away
The dewy ink in tendril fumes.

In Bramble Dell, the beetles played croquet.
They knocked round seeds through leafy hoops,
And sent them all a-bumble down the green.
I ringed their course in lazy loops.

I saw a train of ants in hearty march
To brittle snap of acorn drum.
Their leader, busby-topped and crimson-clad,
Fifed out a tune for them to hum.

They freighted goods in swelling burlap bags,
Tugged mounded carts of flax and grain.
Up tree, down stone, up weed and poppy stem,
So went their unrelenting train.

At last, the Oat Field. Morning's lancing beams
Dispersed the whirlpools of the night,
Coaxed forth staccato songs from warming chaff,
Lit yellow acres wide and bright.

On Royal Mountain stood a quiet man
Before an empty canvas wall.
He made a thumbprint on the air, then eyed
The sheer-faced tower, dizzy-tall.

I signaled with a flourish of my wings.
"Riloo!" I cried. But did he hear?
His answer was a smoke ring sketched on air.
It wafted up. I circled near.

His trousers bleached by noon-high hammock bronze,
His shirt a cloud as soft as down,
All tabby-striped and dandelion-gray,
A jade-green feather in his crown,

He smelled of rhubarb pie and washtub suds
And buttered peas and cheese and gin.
His corncob smokestack twitched in musing lips.
Fine whiskers dusted sandstone chin.

He held a platter gummed with linseed swamp,
The sampled hues of twenty climes,
From ochre putties scooped from forest deeps
To toadstool gums and silver slimes.

He dawdled through the sludge with hairy wand,
Through gully ooze and amber clays.
He snaked a valley through the oily bog,
And mingled mud a hundred ways.

He tickled canvas, blinked, and cocked his head.
A sundial flashed. The canvas blurred.
He flickered nimble strokes with bird-quick hand.
The crackling Oatland Forest stirred.

I felt a breeze beguile me from my course.
I tossed amid its artful draw.
The charge of summer lighting pricked my wings.
I spun, and reeled at what I saw:

In sunken Barn I once explored a cave,
The famed "Kaleidoscope." It's true:
Within its mirror-maze another barn
Is neatly folded through and through.

The canvas turned Kaleidoscope just then,
He smeared his muds to form a view:
A symmetry of houses circus-stacked
Through tilted rows of cowslip blue.

The canvas disappeared, and through its frame
I saw the meadow-tale retold,
The house on Royal Mountain built anew
And every oat, now dipped in gold.

And after I had left the scene behind
My eye retained its dazzled flare.
In rake, in pail, in stone, in stack of hay,
Kaleidoscopes were everywhere.

All told, Nellerelium bowed a nimble bow from atop his scepter perch. The Queen commended him. A whirlwind of applause on all sides. The beetles stamped their nettle-spears and shouted, "Huzzah!"

The Queen yawned. The bluebells took this as their signal and began their jingle, lightly. The insect-soldiers marched away. The wrens dispersed.

The Queen closed her eyes, and slept.

CHAPTER 21

A PAGE REVEALED

The whole time Heather spoke, it was all Milton could do to keep himself from interrupting to ask the dozen questions that burned within him. He wanted to ask: When a painting was finished and Jonathan had gone to sleep, did you ever stand there alone, just looking into the landscape? Did you ever watch the Oat Field, and see the ripples move through it? Did you ever stand very still, close your eyes, and feel it, and feel the same breeze that combs the night grasses and hurls Nellerelium about reach out and chill your face?

But he didn't dare.

He said all the safe, polite things about what a marvelous story it was, and how marvelous it must have been to live there that summer, and how much he enjoyed her telling of it. But the dozen questions still burned.

(Did you happen to see a pantalooned Pierrot somersaulting over the hills, a paper lantern following him like a dog?)

Heather was quiet now, still ambling in recollection, sketching nonsense on the ground with a lanky stick.

Did you ever step through?

She sketched. He studied her marks, studied his shoes, studied the beech trees reaching up, looking for some escape. (Why do I want to escape? Because I've found someone too good to be true? Because I've found the perfect guide, and I don't want to say something foolish to upset her and lose her? She's my only hope for finding Larking Land, and she's right beside me, and this whole plan is so fragile, but here she is, and she's taking me there, and she says it's not far. It's all so precious, like a shivering bubble that can burst on anything. I could find Lorien tomorrow or I could burst the bubble and lose her forever. Oh God, Thulemander, please stay away. Not now. Don't come back now.)

Milton silently fretted.

(I want to whisper everything in her ear. I want to tell her about Lampyridae and Braymouth and the ships on Thistle Bay, and how I tried to find Lorien in the ruins, and there was only charred frames and rubbish and everything burnt, and here she is not two inches from me, and my lips won't move. What am I doing wrong? Why can't I tell her these things?)

Firstly, because there was just too much to tell. Where would he begin? How could he begin? He couldn't remember any beginning. Larking Land had gone on as long as he could remember. It was like picking up a pen and sitting down to write out your life story from first to last. The first blank page will swallow you up.

But she must have been to Larking Land herself. Knowing that changed everything.

Where could he start? What little piece could he give her?

She sketched. He watched. She looked up from her doodling only once, as if she expected Milton might speak. A patient look. Something about the look stirred something in Milton that would not settle. He fidgeted.

The doodle grew elaborate.

Milton mumbled something about a snowy walk he had taken a long time ago.

"Tell me about it," Heather said.

And he told a very short story about strolling down Tillington Road, and of little things that he had noticed along the way, how the snow crunched and squeaked beneath his feet, the windows were glass scored with frost like a pie crust, there were powdered-sugar shutters on the old stone houses, and other things.

Heather listened, anxious to see where the walk would lead. When it didn't lead anywhere, and Milton's story trailed off into his staring again at his shoes, she said that the stroll sounded lovely. She erased her doodles in the dirt, and they resumed their walk.

Milton hardly spoke all the rest of the afternoon. He trailed behind Heather, keeping a safe distance. He could not pull his mind away from the anecdote he had told. It gnawed at him. Why?

Because he had stolen it. It was a page from the Book of Days.

But the book belonged to him, didn't it?

Yes, but also to *her,* to Lorien.

He had given up a secret. He had torn a page from the Book of Days and given it to a stranger.

Would Lorien ever forgive him for that?

He didn't know. It worried him.

It was just a single page. No harm in that, was there?

Would the Book of Days allow that? Or would the pages blacken and shrivel up? Would they crumble at his touch into dust? If they did, would Lorien ever forgive him?

Lorien, he whispered to the hills. *I'm sorry. It was just a peek. Just a glimpse. She seems so innocent, and I didn't think it could hurt. I just didn't think.*

The hills did not answer.

Lorien, I'm sorry.

Still no answer. He lagged so far behind that Heather appeared a mere stick figure on the horizon, no larger than the poppies near his feet. The afternoon, which never could decide whether to give in to full day or languish into a blustery twilight of clouds, finally abandoned daylight altogether and dropped veils of purple clouds everywhere. Heather nearly disappeared now in their midst, a gilded ship adrift in fog. (What if I just stopped here? What if I just stopped and let everything overgrow me like an old fence? Would Heather turn back and look for me? Would she recognize me, all overgrown like that?)

Before he could explore the question even for himself, he saw something tracing luminous lines on the air in an erratic cursive: a single firefly. Then another, and another, and now a swarm of fireflies swirled into a ball, which became a paper lamp that began a drowsy orbit around a pantalooned Pierrot who had risen from behind the nearby hillock, tilting and tipping this way and that, all the while applauding so heartily that the sound ricocheted through the valley like a volley of tiny firecrackers.

"Bravo, Milton, bravo!"

Milton's heart leaped.

"Lampyridae!"

He ran toward the revolving man, but in the blink of an eye he had vanished, and taken his lamp with him. Upon reaching the hillock, all Milton found were a few fireflies that had been left behind. He called out to Lampyridae, but no one answered. He looked in all directions for the dim moon bobbing on some horizon, but saw only half-dissolved mountain ranges in the distance. He tried to catch a firefly, but they eluded him effortlessly.

For a moment, it didn't matter. For a moment, the sight of them was enough. They danced a lightning ninny-dance before him. He chuckled.

Oh, Lorien, please forgive me!

CHAPTER 22

INQUIRIES

The quiet little inn was the last place Heather would have expected to find a Constable, much less an Inspector, yet upon returning from their walk she found one of each in conference with the innkeeper, who clearly had not expected to find them either. She had the impression by the way he shrank under their scrutiny that the Law had never darkened the door of his humble hostelry, and now that the shadow had arrived, he could not fathom what business could have brought it here. The Law asked questions. The innkeeper answered, always in discreet tones, as though speaking any louder might attract further trouble. As the inquiry persisted he grew pinched and white, and he began to steal little worried glances at Heather and look back at the Law as if to beg mercy. He pointed a timid finger in her direction.

The Inspector thanked the innkeeper, took leave of him, and turned toward Heather.

"Pardon me, miss. You are Miss Heather Gabrielle Feur-De-Lys?"

Heather said she was.

"Inspector Smith, Slackington Police Force. This is Constable Colby. We would like to have a word with you, if we may."

Inspector Smith explained that he was in charge of finding missing persons, and that he was at present looking for a particular missing person by the name of one Mr. Jacob Hartshorne; that certain parties (unnamed) who had a vested interest in finding him had charged him with that duty, and that he (the Inspector) was presently making inquiries of all who knew him, in order that he might locate him; that he had, in the course of his inquiries, ascertained that Miss Feur-De-Lys was a regular acquaintance of Mr. Jacob Hartshorne, who might know his present whereabouts, or, if she didn't know them, might at least hold some clue valuable in deducing them; that he would like to put a few questions to her which might provide him with said clues, if she could spare a few minutes; and pardon the inconvenience of it all. Could she grant him and his colleague an interview, immediately?

Heather said she supposed she could.

The Constable eyed Milton, then Heather, as if to ask whether she would prefer to conduct this interview in private. By way of reply, Heather briefly introduced Milton, and they all sat down. She asked how she could be of help.

Thanking her for her cooperation, the Inspector produced a notepad, cleared his throat, and began.

"When was the last time you saw Mr. Hartshorne?"

Heather thought for a moment.

"Well, I didn't exactly see him, but I heard him some months ago, in the tunnel beneath the theatre. Do you know about the tunnels?"

(A little embarrassment.) "I'm afraid I don't. Pray tell me."

"There was originally a castle on the site, fallen into ruin. When the grounds were cleared away to build the theatre, tunnels were found beneath the castle. Perhaps there used to be a dungeon. No one really knows. The architects sealed the tunnels shut, and everybody forgot about them. Then recently I discovered—quite by accident—that the tunnels had been reopened.

"I had stayed in the theatre late one night—after midnight, I think. Everyone had gone home. I had decided to stay and read through some new songs. I had just sorted through my music when I heard a dreadful sound coming from somewhere in one of the other rooms. A muffled shouting, or wailing. It rose in one horrible crescendo, then died away.

"I tried to return to my work, but the silence was still tainted by an echo of that sound. Where I should have heard the written melodies, I heard only that awful cry, rising up and then trailing away.

"I forced myself to concentrate on the notes, and for the space of four or five pages everything except my music disappeared, and I was safe.

"Then the wailing swelled up again and flooded through the emptiness, worse this time.

"I have always felt at home in theatres at night, ever since I was a little girl. When I was very young I thought that when the actors had all gone home, their characters remained somewhere backstage, packed away in the wardrobe room perhaps, or sleeping among the properties, or roaming invisible through the empty halls waiting to don their actors like robes when they returned. It might sound silly, but I suppose that notion never completely left me, because to this day, in the silence of the night theatre, I don't feel alone.

"Wasn't it only natural that the wailing made me think of the characters all pent up somewhere, rattling some cage where they found themselves trapped? When I heard that cry, it was as if Pandora had opened Shakespeare's Box of Tragedies, and loosed all its victims to shriek their terrors at the world. For the first time, I began to dread the silence of the night theatre.

"And yet, would you believe that some morbid curiosity pulled me toward the voice? I had to know if it was real—and, if it was, who was in so much pain.

"I stepped into the hall. I could tell the wailing was coming from a room toward the far end, Mr. Hartshorne's room.

"I crept softly.

"I knocked on his door.

"Nobody answered.

"'Mr. Hartshorne?' I said, a little too quietly. No one answered.

"My hand trembled on the doorknob.

"The door was unlocked. I dared to peep into the room. No one.

"I don't know why I looked. My heart was racing and told me to run away, but something stronger pulled me into that room, and toward that terrible voice."

At this the Inspector looked incredulous. "You ventured into this room by yourself?"

Heather nodded.

"You did not call for help?"

She shook her head.

The Inspector seemed impressed. "Most extraordinary. Pray continue."

"It was lit by a single candle flickering upon a desk wild with papers and smeared ink. I smelled stale wine, and saw the glimmer of several empty bottles abandoned on various shelves and on the desk. I didn't see anyone, but there was a door on the far wall. It was wide open. Had it not been, I would have mistaken it for a wall. It appeared as smooth stone, as though it had been intended as a secret passageway. I remembered then that Mr. Hartshorne had overseen the repairing of the theatre, and guessed that he had for some reason devised a means to the old tunnels to provide him a secret enclave, though I could not guess why. It opened into a cool dark passage with a crumbling floor. The farther I went, the more twisted the tunnels became. I followed it only a little way, until I heard the wailing again, so close now I could not mistake it: the voice of Mr. Hartshorne.

"It's uncanny the way you can read meanings in the cadences of a voice. Now I could follow every rise and fall of Hartshorne's voice, and without catching more than a broken phrase here or there, I knew that his lament took the form of a pleading. I didn't know who he was pleading to, or why, but I imagined him fretting before the bench of some imperious judge, throwing himself at his mercy but gaining not an inch of ground toward winning his favors, no matter what ploy he tried. The voice shook, and I was certain I would hear the judge's gavel hammer him down to nothing, but the voice only shrank away. After a heavy silence it returned to continue its plea.

"Although the whole time I listened I could make out only a few words, I did discern two themes that he kept repeating, that seemed to be his main defense: He kept saying, in one form or another, that he was sorry for what he had done, and that he had been terribly cold. I didn't know what to make of that, and still don't, but I can still hear that litany cried out again and again, in vain.

"'Terribly cold, terribly cold!'

"I ran.

"I ran silently but swiftly back through the halls to my room, gathered my things, and rushed toward the backstage door.

"I sped through the night street, glancing only once over my shoulder to assure myself that I wasn't being followed. A beggar called out to me from his shelter in a door frame, and for a moment I mistook him for Hartshorne. Once safe inside the inn, I awoke Philippe.

"I have awakened him from enough late-night slumbers that he normally thinks nothing of it, and bothers no more than to light a candle, raise his eyelids only to half-mast, and nod at everything I say. But he must have sensed my urgency that night: he threw on his robe, built a small fire, and listened to me. As I told my story his face deepened with grave attention, and when I ended it he sank back in his chair, silent.

"He had known Mr. Hartshorne nearly as long as I, so the absurdity of my experience was so striking that it robbed him of words. Only after half a cigarette did he put forth his theory of what may have happened in the tunnel:

"Philippe guessed that Mr. Hartshorne used this secret enclave to meet some partner there and conduct some unscrupulous business, and that Mr. Hartshorne had blundered in some plan the two of them had made, and was defending himself that night, possibly fearing the retribution his partner-in-crime might deliver. It would certainly explain his hysteria.

"But it did not explain why I only heard one voice, I pointed out. Did the other speak in low, conspiratorial tones? Or was Hartshorne simply mad and babbling to the walls?

"What were we to do?

"We discussed telling the police, then, but Philippe thought that would be meddling. We could not prove any crime, or even prove that any business meeting had ever happened, and though I didn't believe Philippe's theory, I deferred to his judgment to leave the matter alone.

"When Philippe and I walked the same street back to the theatre the next morning, I saw that the light of day had boiled away the phantoms of the previous night. The theatre, too, now buzzing with activity, seemed purged of all its foreboding. My night's ordeal paled like a bad dream.

"But I did not see Mr. Hartshorne. I think that was the last time I saw him."

The Inspector had taken copious notes.

"Miss Feur-De-Lys, you are quite adventuresome. This is a most extraordinary account, and yet, I must confess, it is all most perplexing. Is there anything you could tell us that might shed some light upon this mystery of the tunnel? Did you notice Mr. Hartshorne acting in any way peculiar, prior to this incident? Do you know of any episode in his history that might give us some clue?"

Heather turned the incident over in her mind, and all she could think about were the broken phrases. It had been terribly cold, Mr. Hartshorne had said. When she searched back through the years that she had known him, she did find one winter that had been longer and much more cruel than the rest, and she could taste the bitter crystals stinging the air as she walked again through the long white month that had indeed touched something deep inside Mr. Jacob Hartshorne. Wasn't that when it had begun to happen? Wasn't that the winter into which he had disappeared and never quite returned?

"Well, yes, I do remember one incident, a long time ago," she said, "although I don't know just how to describe it. I don't really know where to begin."

"Start from the beginning," the Inspector said simply. "Perhaps if you give us a brief account of your history with Mr. Hartshorne, it might bring to light certain clues. No detail is too small, Miss Feur-De-Lys. Anything you can relate is potentially useful."

Heather resumed her story.

CHAPTER 23

THE TALE OF
MR. HARTSHORNE

"I've known Hartshorne for years. He was an admirer of my mother, and they were good friends. Mr. Hartshorne used to attend all of my mother's performances, both here and in London, and he attended my performances as well. He was an ardent patron of the arts. When he bought this theatre and supervised the repairs, he did so not merely by pointing or drawing up charts and diagrams. He picked up a hammer and led the way with all the fervor of a young Michelangelo. His own woodworking skills amazed his colleagues, and when he had completed the work, architects, craftsmen, and interior designers traveled down from London to see the Hartshorne Theatre (as it was called then). It had become the showpiece of Slackington.

"Being so well acquainted with him, I had the privilege to see a more intimate creation, a special room which he had designed within his own estate. Among his circle of friends, it had garnered a fame of its own, and had become so special to me in my childhood that I had invented skipping-rope rhymes in homage to it, and taught them to my playmates. It really was a very special room.

"He used to give parties—small ones, luncheons, dinners and such—and after our meal and a little conversation, he would show us his special room. Though I dared not misbehave in Mr. Hartshorne's house, I could hardly keep from squirming with impatience through all the after-dinner talk when I knew that the room was just around the corner. Drink, drink! I'd think to myself. Finish your tea, and finish your talking so we can leave this boring table and go to the room. Don't you know what awaits us? Hurry! Let's go!

"The Enchanted Forest.

"That is exactly what it was: a room made entirely of wood, from the carved paneled walls to the polished mahogany floor and everything in between, all fashioned to resemble some fanciful woodland of Hartshorne's own creation. An immense oak table appeared to grow out of an enormous tree stump. Ivy crept up the sideboard in thick tendrils. The floor was inlaid to resemble the thick leaf-carpet of a forest floor, and the walls were fluted with tree trunks which hid amid their depths a variety of creatures. It became a great game to search for them and point them out. I remember my delight at first discovering them one by one (Mr. Hartshorne never revealed them, but always let his guests find them on their own). I looked to the north wood: a hare twitched his nose at me. I looked to the south wood: a centaur squinted shrewdly, hairy arms folded. I looked east and west, and saw thrushes and wrens. I looked again: a gnome held a finger to

his lips, then winked at me, as if to ask that I keep his secret and not give his hiding place away.

"Have you ever felt a room to be as big as the whole world? Well, that was the effect of Hartshorne's Enchanted Forest. The walls seemed to dissolve away, and soon the woodland was everywhere, and you could smell the decayed leaves beneath your feet and hear the cool murmur of a brook somewhere, and the scamper of squirrels above you in the boughs. It was like taking a little journey. Before I knew it I was sipping from that cool brook, then washing my face, then falling asleep to the hum of the waters winding through the lush ravines. I had the impression that Mr. Hartshorne made a similar journey whenever he visited the room. Sometimes I would catch him: in the midst of company, during some idle moment when the spotlight had turned away from himself as a host, he appeared to slip away for a moment into his own personal forest, until the distant voice of a guest would call him back.

"I could have sat in that room forever.

"I imagine that Mr. Hartshorne could have as well. He looked like the forest. The forest looked like him. I had never seen him more at home than when he brought us there, took his seat in his oaken throne (a rocking chair), and hid himself in wry silence while we all revolved in awe, pointing and exclaiming in hushed tones. No matter how many times I explored it, I always found something new, a newly etched starling here, a dwarf whittled in there, so that I never knew what I might discover.

"I tell you all this so you will understand my shock when I returned to Hartshorne's estate years later, after the terrible winter in sixty-eight. I can no better explain it now than I could then, but I know that was the winter that Mr. Hartshorne changed.

"Do you remember the storm, Inspector? It buried the whole town, all but the church steeple. Mr. Hartshorne's is up on Baretop Hill, near the summit, and when the snows came and buried the only road to his estate, he was cut off from Slackington, from the world.

"You could imagine that, with all the mayhem, I was not surprised to learn that Hartshorne had failed to appear at the theatre, and that nobody knew his whereabouts. Nobody knew *anyone's* whereabouts! I presumed he was tending to some crisis of his own, as everyone else was, and thought nothing more of it. As soon as the roads permitted my escape, I took the next coach back to London to perform at the Alhambra and didn't return to Slackington until nearly five months later, in late March. By then most of the ice had melted away, and I had thought that everything in Slackington had returned to normal.

"I was wrong.

"When I visited the theatre, I learned that Mr. Hartshorne still had not returned. Gossip buzzed in the hushed clusters of actors and stagehands in the wings and dressing rooms, so I could not help but catch wind of the rumor—but neither could I believe it. Why should I? Backstage gossip was as common as greasepaint, and just as thin. Scrub it with a damp towel and it washes away, does it not? I wouldn't have given it a second thought, except this was the wrong kind of gossip. It did not flow freely between seamstresses sewing or stagehands setting up scenery, but only broke out in worried little knots that dispersed before anyone could savor anything. They spoke it as though saying it too loud might deliver the same fate upon them: their voices grew thin and short, and caught in their throats.

"Rumor had it that Mr. Hartshorne had been snowed in at his estate for five months, alone, and that the prolonged isolation had driven him insane.

"According to the rumor, Mr. Dirth himself (who was then the bookkeeper) had called on Mr. Hartshorne directly after the storm to see how he had fared. Some hideous exchange had occurred between them, but since the reports already varied from one telling to the next, I couldn't be sure which was true, if any. Though I was inclined not to believe any of it, the talk troubled me enough to ask Mr. Dirth himself just what he had seen and what he had said, which had started such rumors.

"I found Mr. Dirth in his office, balancing the books. His jaunty air had been crushed by some oppressive weight that bent him and brought out all the hollows of his face. The whimsical lilt of his lips had left him, and his complexion had gone pasty.

"'What's wrong?' I asked.

"'What makes you ask?' he countered. 'Nothing!' He tried to shoo me away with a flurry of his arm, but of course it wouldn't do. After I pulled him out of his papers and made clear I would not go away, he listened as I told him the gossip I had heard about his visit to Mr. Hartshorne's house.

"'Is any of it true?' I asked.

"Mr. Dirth winced with regret. 'I never should have breathed a word of it to anyone. Please, just forget the whole thing!' He tried to retreat again into his ledger.

"'Do you know what they are saying? Did you hear the part about his chasing you out with a hot poker?'

"A reply crept up his throat. He swallowed it back down.

"'Mr. Dirth, if these things aren't true, you owe it to Mr. Hartshorne to say so.'

"He came out of his ledger looking very stern. 'Miss Feur-De-Lys, I have seen rumors spread like cholera throughout a theatrical company. It can divide them, and promote factions, pettiness, and discontent. Do you think I would serve Mr. Hartshorne by tearing him down in the eyes of his company? Take it from me, these matters are best diffused by laying low. Ignore a rumor, and it will go away. But breathe a word of it to anyone—' he finished with a shudder.

"'You can at least tell *me*. Is any of it true?'

"He asked me to let the matter rest. Then he buried himself in his papers, and would not come out. But he didn't need to. The way his last words grew thin and caught in his throat told me that something of the rumors was true. I think he knew that I had puzzled that out, because for the rest of our conversation (which amounted to nothing), he could not look me in the eye.

"I decided to pay Mr. Hartshorne a visit. A surprise visit. (I know that this is highly irregular, Inspector, but you must understand, I had known him since I was a child. How could I let him disappear like this? I couldn't.)

"I took a coach up to his estate, which was now accessible, though the walls of snow remained on either side of the road piled nearly as tall as the coach itself in places. They formed a long white corridor which even in the afternoon sun showed no signs of melting. The glare of the sun on those walls nearly blinded me.

"At the end of the road was Mr. Hartshorne's house, still half-glazed in ice.

"No footman answered when I rang the bell. Rumor had it that the servants had been fired. Evidently, that much was true.

"I rang again. Still no answer.

"I peeked in a window. Darkness.

"'Mr. Hartshorne?' My words fogged the air. No reply.

"I tried the door. It was unlocked.

"I knew that if I was going to find out the truth about Mr. Hartshorne, I would have to discover it myself. And wasn't it my duty to find out? Until I saw it with my own eyes, I wouldn't know what to believe. And I had to do *something*.

"I let myself in. (I simply *had* to!)

"I suppose I had *really* come to disprove the rumors, which was why I was so upset at what I saw. I almost turned right back around and marched out, but I had come this far, and I had to know the rest.

"The house looked dreadful.

"Mostly, it was empty, or nearly so. The dining-room table was gone. The sideboard was gone. All the chairs were gone. From the look of the place I would have thought that he had moved out, except that a few items remained—a candlestick, a mirror. If he were leaving I should have expected to find all his things boxed up, or perhaps the entire contents of one room gone, but not another, yet I couldn't find any rhyme or reason in what was missing and what remained. I did notice that all the furniture he had made himself was gone. Strange.

"But that was not nearly as strange as the coal.

"Beside the fireplace he had dumped a tremendous pile of coal, and next to it, several barrels brimmed over with more—far more than he could ever need to heat a house that size through any winter. I could only guess that he had overfilled his basement and kept the extra there next to the fireplace (which was filthy black) for lack of space, but it was still far more coal than I could sensibly account for.

"Perhaps Mr. Hartshorne's reason for amassing it went beyond all sense.

"That gave me a shudder.

"I knew I couldn't leave without checking one more room.

"*Please,* I thought, *please*.

"I touched the door, put my ear to it, hoping against hope to hear him. Of all the retreats he could possibly have run to, wouldn't he come back to this one? I imagined him sitting in his great oak chair, smoking his cigar in that same old wry silence, talking back to the squirrels that clowned above him on their branchwork tightropes.

"Almost without thinking, his name came to my lips. I whispered: 'Mr. Hartshorne?'

"From within, a rhythmic creaking.

"Again, very soft: 'Mr. Hartshorne?'

"Still, the rhythmic creaking—his rocking chair.

"'Mr. Hartshorne, I'm sorry to have disturbed you by coming unannounced, but I was a little concerned. I heard . . . I heard you were not well, so I came to visit you to see if I could help in some way.'

"*Creak, creak.*

"I tried to think of what to say next, but everything sounded wrong. I kept framing questions in my mind, but backing away from them.

"I thought: What can happen in a winter, all alone? What phantom could come and haunt you, numb you with his touch? There is snow and quiet and all the time in the world to read and whittle and dream up new landscapes. It would be a sanctuary, would it not? A little hibernation?

"*Creak, creak.*

"What can happen in a winter, all alone, Jacob? I thought. The servants had left and the storm set in and buried you in ten feet of snow, and here you were. Weren't you safe? Didn't you still have the forest, the woods and knolls to roam through? And didn't they go on forever?

"But all I said was, 'Mr. Hartshorne? Jacob?'

"*Creak, creak.*

"You still had your chisel, you still had your knife, you still had everything you needed to be Jacob Hartshorne and whittle up your own summer there within the winter, rich with all sorts of foxes and squirrels and doves to keep you company through any winter, Jacob, any winter. No frost can penetrate these trees, no snow can petrify them. Please say something.

" 'Jacob?' I repeated.

"*Creak, creak.*

"I see you in there, Jacob, I thought, a little man sitting in a large oak chair, embattled by the icicles barring the window, but still warm in the heart of your own glade, warm and protected. A little man, shrunken, but still safe and sound and dreaming and whittling, and not insane, not insane at all, just shaken by a winter that lasted a little too long. Jacob, please speak to me.

"I decided to try another approach:

" 'Jacob? I never told you this, but when I was a little girl, you were the only adult besides my mother that I ever trusted. I mean, this whole place, this whole forest—when I saw this, I knew you understood. You weren't like the other grown-ups. You talked differently. I used to look forward to seeing this room and this place. And do you know what? I still do. I look forward to it just as much as when I was a little girl.'

"Wasn't there always a bit of the child in him? Wasn't that where all those worlds came from?

" 'You know, sometimes when I sing and the footlights are so bright I can't see anything, and I lose my place in the music, I think about your forest, and the way it felt to walk through it, and sometimes, if I concentrate very hard, everything falls into place. The blindness of the lights makes everything else disappear, and just for a moment, I'm back here, walking through the forest, singing. I'm sure you never guessed that, did you, Jacob?'

"*Creak, creak.*

" 'Please open the door, Jacob.'

"*Creak, creak.*

" 'Jacob, I'm coming in now, all right?'

"I eased the door open.

"The Enchanted Forest was gone.

"The wooden paneling had all been stripped off. Not a single panel remained. The exposed wall studs bore ragged nail teeth. A crowbar had pried away sections of the ceiling. Several floorboards had been torn out as well, and the sections that remained had been scarred and gouged by rough heels or dragging chair legs.

"All the furniture was gone.

"All except one piece: The rocking chair.

"The wind came in through the broken window in gusts that tossed the empty rocking chair to and fro on the torn and creaking floor.

"I felt sick.

"I left the room.

"I left the house, and never returned."

The Inspector scratched his head in frustration. "You have no theory as to what drove him to tear up the room?"

"No, I haven't," said Heather.

"When did you actually see Hartshorne again?"

"During one of my performances, the last one he ever attended. He took his usual seat in the balcony box, and I could see him quite plainly. I don't know whether he knew I could see him—audiences have this curious notion that there is some mysterious wall between them and us—but I could see him all right. I remember seeing him leave that night. He left abruptly, in the middle of my performance, not as though someone had called him away, but as though he was simply disgusted and couldn't listen any more. I've seen that irate sort of departure many times, from critics and such. (I don't know if you are aware, Inspector, but my repertoire is very modern, and in some circles, very controversial.) Mr. Hartshorne, offended? He had attended my performances since I was ten years old. Yet I could neither mistake nor deny that disgusted lurch of the shoulders as he stormed through the curtain of the box and disappeared.

"That curtain stirred through the rest of the song, like the ripples in a lake where a man has fallen in and disappeared beneath the surface. It chilled me.

"I never saw him at my performances after that. Every night I would look out of the corner of my eye at his balcony box, and every night, it was empty, its curtain disturbingly still.

"On the few occasions I saw him from a distance, attending business in the theatre or about town, the man I saw was not Mr. Hartshorne. I watched a stranger walking in Mr. Hartshorne's shoes but doing things Mr. Hartshorne would never do, and saying things he would never say. Others, too, commented that he 'was not himself.' But in time, those comments began to die out, because the man who *had* been Mr. Hartshorne began to fade from everyone's memory. Few had seen the Enchanted Forest, and those who had, apparently had forgotten it, and forgotten the man who had made it. But I did not forget.

"My impression was that the real Mr. Hartshorne never really did emerge from his house that winter. He was still trapped in there.

"I watched the man who was not Hartshorne become a businessman, investing in the chain- and nail-making trade. He pursued it fervently, not with the old Michelangelo fervor, but more like a locomotive, all iron barreling and pouring off steam. I saw it in the way he walked through the streets, clenching a cigar between his teeth and seeing no one as he elbowed his way through the crowds. Before long, people learned to get out of his way when they saw him coming. The street urchins would scatter, and beggars knew better than to ask him for a farthing, or even to look at him.

"I heard he did well in the metalwork trade, but I never heard of him carving wood or, indeed, making anything with his hands again—and that worried me. He became obsessed with his new business. I heard rumors about how it drove him relentlessly and fueled wicked fits of temper when anything threatened to distract him. I heard that his campaign to raise new funds had reached an unparalleled fury. This pursuit took him further and further away from his former concerns, until the theatre began to fall into a state of disrepair. But still, I was shocked when I returned there one day to discover his team of carpenters scaling the walls with ropes and ladders, and attacking the decorated friezes with hammers, crowbars, and chisels.

"Naturally, I demanded an explanation.

"'Gave the order just last week, miss,' said the rather grimy figure I had accosted. 'We're to strip all these here walls of all what's gold, so as he can sell it. Found a buyer up London way. Goldsmith. Needs raw materials, he does.' He attacked a scroll with a hammer.

"'But why?' I demanded. 'Why tear it all down?'

"'Can't say, miss. Don't know. If you want my guess, I'd say it's money he wants, pure and simple.

He's a shrewd businessman, this one, and ruthless. Theatre doesn't make enough money, down it goes, one piece at a time.'

"I stormed out.

"A few weeks later I discovered the tunnel, and Mr. Hartshorne, wailing.

"Several times I hailed a coach with the intent of calling on him again at his estate, but each time I waved the coach away at the last minute. Several times I passed the door to his office and glanced in as I passed, afraid to look too closely. It was always empty.

"No, come to think of it, that was not the last time I saw him. There was the night he threw me out.

"I was not as distressed by the fact that he had canceled my contract as I was by the way that he had done it. He did not talk to me in person, or even to Philippe. Instead, he sent Mr. Dirth to tell Philippe. By sending a deputy, he had put enough distance between himself and the crime that he could pretend he had nothing to do with it, or even pretend it had never happened—but of course, Philippe snuffed that fiction before it took flame. He stormed into Mr. Hartshorne's office in a passion and had words with him, which had achieved nothing, except to allow me to finish my last scheduled show (which I performed only last week). I was not to return next season. Though Philippe never told me exactly what had transpired during their argument, I know he never did get any reason for my dismissal out of Mr. Hartshorne. When he came back, he looked defeated.

"'Save your voice,' he said when I began to object. 'It's no use.' He said it like a doctor talking of a patient who was beyond his help. It was not like Philippe to speak that way. He began explaining the whole thing away with his theory about a conspiracy that had somehow ensnared Mr. Hartshorne, but I still didn't believe it, and I told him so.

"'Then what do you believe?' he asked.

"I didn't know what to think.

"The first performance I ever gave was on that stage, when I was ten. This was the first theatre I had ever really known, and the thought of leaving it and never coming back seemed impossible.

"After speaking to Philippe, I stayed somewhat late that night. The stage was empty, so I decided to rehearse onstage, for old time's sake.

"I sang.

"I started with purring, then moved on to descending sighs, then progressed to scales, and then to a few run-throughs of a melody I have sung for many years. On the highest crescendos I could hear the overtones ring back from the hollows of the balconies, just as they should. The melody was beginning to come alive.

" 'Tell her to stop that awful singing!' another voice crashed in from behind me.

"There was a dumb-struck pause, then a frantic mumbling.

" 'No, Mr. Dirth, I do *not* like it. I never *did* like it! She's canceled, now get rid of her! Tell her to stop!'

"A door slammed a mile off backstage.

"Mr. Dirth came onstage moving as if in a dream. Some horror had wrung him and blanched him and frayed him at the ends. He could hardly speak.

" 'I'm terribly sorry, Miss Feur-De-Lys,' he sputtered.

"I left the stage.

"I walked backstage between the rows of moldy scenery flats and fragments of sets, and I thought of going back to Mr. Hartshorne's door and knocking very gently, and whispering his name, and seeing who came out. Before I could even gather my courage to do so, I heard his footfalls. He passed me on his way out into the night.

"That was the last time I saw him, that night when he left the theatre. He left with that same disgusted lurch of the shoulders that I had seen when he left in the middle of my performance, with this difference. In the one brief glimpse I caught of his face, I saw something I had half expected, yet out of hope had half denied, but could now no longer deny. This man was not Jacob Hartshorne. There was not a trace of the Enchanted Forest in this face, not the merest hint. He gave not the slightest sign of recognition. In fact, he gave no attempt at recognition at all. He did not look upon me as though I were a stranger. He looked *through* me, then passed me as though I were not there."

CHAPTER 24

THE GOLDEN CHILD

"You never saw Mr. Hartshorne after this incident?" asked the Inspector.

"That was the last time," said Heather. "He sold the theatre just recently, you know, to Mr. Dirth and Mr. Brim. He doesn't visit the theatre anymore."

After jotting a few more notes, the Inspector stopped writing and began tapping the pad, as though working on some incalculable sum. In a moment, he arrived not at an answer but another request, which he made to Heather.

"Miss Feur-De-Lys, may I ask your further assistance? I think it's time we took a look in Mr. Hartshorne's secret tunnel."

The Inspector was not one to let the grass grow beneath his feet. No sooner did he say it than the four of them hailed a coach. The two policemen, Heather, and Milton raced to Dirth and Brim's Company Theatre, then backstage, and into Mr. Hartshorne's office, only to be faced with a tall, obstinate barrier that stopped them in their tracks: a door.

Locked.

"It was not locked before?" asked the Inspector.

"No," said Heather.

The Constable produced a set of picks from within his coat, and set to work. Soon there was a click, the Constable tried the latch, and the door swung open.

The Inspector tried to discourage Heather from accompanying them, to no avail. Her insistence won him over and he conceded, appointing her lantern bearer. But he warned her, and Milton, too: they were treading on treacherous ground. Hartshorne was a dangerous man, and whomever he met in this hideout when he conducted his secret interviews was no doubt more dangerous still. This enclave smacked of the organized crime rings of the Underworld, the Inspector was sure of it, and he was certain that Hartshorne through some shady business must have become mixed up in their ranks.

"Beware," he said. "At the least sign of danger, retreat, and leave this matter to us."

This warning did not have near as much impact on Milton as did the sight of the pistols. The Inspector produced two from within his greatcoat, armed his Constable, and readied his weapon before turning to the dry mouth of the tunnel. Milton felt his blood run cold, but he couldn't back out now and leave Heather (who seemed undaunted by the guns). He brought up the rear.

The Constable went first, pistol drawn, then the Inspector, then Heather, then Milton. Heather held a bull's-eye lantern high, sending their shadows out to feel their way before them. They entered the tunnel, listening to each other breathe.

The floor was crooked and broken stone, the walls rent with fissures. Cool. Dry. They padded along, finding nothing.

They passed the place where Heather had been stopped by cries, rounded a bend, discovered an empty chamber.

Heather scanned the lantern over every wall, every inch of the floor and ceiling, and both Constable and Inspector combed over all surfaces hunting for clues, but found none.

The tunnel continued.

The party resumed walking, cautiously. The floor now resembled a crumbled staircase in places, descending in short declines, and then it leveled. Down twenty yards or so. Bend to the right. Ten yards, bend to the left. Another door.

This one was bolted, with a crossbar. Could he pick the lock, the Inspector asked the Constable. Not a chance, the Constable replied. They exchanged a look that signified this was very bad.

"Stand back," said the Constable, readying himself as a ram.

He rammed the door. *Slam!*

It bucked, but did not give.

Slam! It bucked again, but still held fast.

Slam! The Constable huffed, rallied, readied his shoulder again. *Slam! Slam!* The Inspector's finger twitched on his pistol. His eyes became eagle-sharp. His face turned to steel.

Slam!

"It's giving way!" shouted the Inspector.

Slam!

"Keep trying!"

Slam!

Crack!

The door burst open.

Another stretch of tunnel. Long. Straight.

Finally, a bend . . .

And another, and another. They crept along slowly. Milton had no idea how far they had gone or which direction they faced or how long it would take him to ricochet back down the yards and miles and centuries of catacomb twistings and ancient stone before he would ever see the theatre again. Should he hear, say, a noise, or see a thug, or something worse . . .

Another bolted door.

"Are you certain this is the right tunnel?" asked the Inspector.

"It's the *only* tunnel," said Heather.

Slam!

"The only tunnel you know of," corrected the Inspector. He gripped his pistol tight.

Slam! Slam! Slam! Crash!

The party rushed in, but immediately halted.

The Inspector lowered his gun.

A craggy enclave, larger than the one before, and within it, a tremendous golden head.

It was the likeness of a child, cast monstrously large. The tops of its curly locks nearly touched the ceiling, a good ten feet high.

The child smiled at them.

The smile struck them all dumb.

"It makes no sense," the Constable finally said. His expression wavered between puzzlement and horror.

The Inspector's eagle eyes combed the Golden Child up and down, reached no conclusion, finally looked about the room in a restless search for clues, but found none. He holstered his pistol and stroked his chin uselessly.

Milton and Heather studied the face of the Golden Child, which looked sublimely back at them. It was too large for a child, unless the child of a giant, and oddly serene in contrast to the consternation of the party.

It was beautiful.

Almost like a cherub, thought Milton. It was a face of innocence, born into a cradle lined with dreams, raised in the heart of a summer country where all roads lead to home, and hidden away in the tunnel for a reason none could guess.

"How the deuce did he convey it in here?" said the Constable.

"I am not half so interested to know *how* he did it," said the Inspector, "as I am to know *why*."

No one offered any answers.

No one even threw out any theories. How could they? The Golden Child simply should not have been there, and for the moment, nothing more could be said about it. A pale Constable and a ruffled Inspector proposed returning to the theatre to rally their resources, and their wits.

The Golden Child smiled.

Milton and Heather elected to remain behind.

The Inspector thanked Miss Feur-De-Lys for her assistance, and said that her tale had proved most singular, most illuminating, yet also most perplexing. He confessed he did not know what to make of the golden head just yet, but he was certain he would make something of it; that such a wealth of data as was provided by her extraordinary account must be rigorously analyzed before he could draw any trustworthy conclusions; that he had no doubt that he would in fact draw said conclusions and thus locate the missing Mr. Hartshorne in due course of time, etc., etc.

Milton suggested that he might try heading northeast, toward Glastonbury, since that was where *he* had last seen Mr. Hartshorne.

The Inspector flared with surprise. When was this?

"Very recently," said Milton.

How recently?

Milton didn't really know. He never carried a watch, so he was not in the habit of noticing what time it was. In his travels, he had similarly lost track of the days.

When the Inspector asked why the deuce he hadn't said anything until now, Milton could only say that he didn't want to interrupt, at which the Inspector bristled, and the Constable narrowed his eyes and folded his arms across his chest. Milton shrank visibly beneath the heat of their glares until Heather broke in with a comment about the urgency of catching up with Mr. Hartshorne before he traveled too far afield, with which both Inspector and Constable agreed. With a formal nod of thanks, the Law excused itself and went off to chase its quarry.

This left Milton and Heather alone with the Golden Child.

Heather stared at the face again, her expression deepening, as though she recognized the face from someplace, but could not remember where.

"The theatre!" she finally said. "Above the stage. That's where I've seen this face. I knew he looked familiar."

Having only seen it in its lofty position of honor above the proscenium, Heather had believed it to be made of gold, or brass. But now they both stepped a little closer to examine the face's complexion, and discovered that the gold was flaked and peeled away in places.

"Gilt wood," said Heather. "He must have carved it himself, then painted it."

The Golden Child smiled. Golden smile. Wooden smile.

"Something dreadful must have happened in his house that winter," she said.

"But that was years ago," said Milton.

"Some things don't go away so easily. One night can change someone."

Milton said he supposed that was true. Still, to tear the head down like that, and then drag it back here in secret and hide it behind barricades, and come back here and talk to it; what could Hartshorne have been thinking?

"Maybe he's carrying around some loss he refuses to mourn, and this is his way of mourning it. Maybe he needs to confess some crime to someone, but is afraid, so this is his way of confessing. People are strange that way. They carry all sorts of things around inside them that they shouldn't."

Milton said he supposed that people were strange.

"He never did tell anyone what happened that winter," said Heather. It was clear to Milton that Heather saw something in the face of the Golden Child that he did not. She approached her discovery slowly, as though she were circling in on something she only dimly perceived.

Milton studied the face of the Golden Child, but found not the slightest resemblance to the Iron Man. No vice-grip tension, no smoldering, no distance in the eyes, only a placid innocence. If the Child could speak, he suspected it would speak only of its dream cradle and the hundred roads toward home. And all this puzzled Milton all the more.

"When you sang that night, and he made you leave," he broached the question carefully, "why do you suppose he did that? Why was he so upset?"

"I don't know, exactly. The funny thing is, the song that sent him into a rage that night was one of his favorite songs. He had swooned over it when he first heard it years ago, in London, I remember. He never knew the lyrics, though I tried to teach him the French once. I suppose he just loved the melody."

Milton was lost even further now. "Can a song be both beautiful and horrible? I mean, how could the same person find so much beauty in a thing, then turn around and call it horrible?"

Heather still searched the face of the Golden Child, homing in.

"Maybe the part of him that heard the beauty is dying," said Heather.

Milton looked aghast. "What makes you say that?"

"I don't know," she said, "except it explains everything so well. It would be like going blind. Imagine waking up one morning and looking at your gallery, and finding the canvasses all blank, then looking out the window to find the hills all drab and drained of color. You would scream, wouldn't you? Or shout at someone, maybe, berate the next person who came along? Of course you would. You'd lash out at everything, because you didn't understand, and you'd be angry and frightened. That's what Mr. Hartshorne is doing, I think, and that's why he made me leave. The song sounded all wrong and empty, and he couldn't bear it."

Milton felt a breath of Mr. Hartshorne's winter touch him. "What could have done that to him?" he asked.

"I don't know," she admitted.

Milton kneeled by the Golden Child. He studied the places where the giltwork had chipped and flaked away to reveal the wood beneath.

Then it struck him.

It was all made of wood.

It had been *cold* that winter.

Suppose Hartshorne had run out of firewood. . . .

Milton thought back to the fire that had consumed Radcliffe House, and suddenly he understood what had happened to Mr. Hartshorne.

He had been the creator and destroyer of a whole world. He had hammered and carved his very own Enchanted Forest out of raw wood, and then burned it as fuel to fend off the cold of a huge, terrible storm. He had survived the winter, but lost his kingdom, and returned to the theatre in disgrace. How could he face his Golden Child and tell it that its father had destroyed their homeland?

He had been carrying the burden of that night around inside him, and it sagged and bent him, hunched him and caved him inward. How could he pick up his tools again without remembering what he had done? How could Hartshorne whittle up the sweet madrigal scrollwork of a new country with the weight of his crime bearing down upon him?

A picture rose in Milton's mind.

He was in the house of Mr. Jacob Hartshorne and the snow was falling, not only outside, but inside as well. Hartshorne was staring into the flames, watching his creations give up their ghosts in bright colors that sparked up the flue, but the fire was not large enough to fend off the cold. The Enchanted Forest crumbled, each fugue of wood twisting and blackening, and something twisted and blackened in Hartshorne's face, something like shame. The snow touched his coat, powdered his hair, his shoulders, flecked his hands. It sifted down into a thin blanket that grew thicker and piled higher and higher, first to his ankles, then his shins, then his knees, until soon it was up to his waist, and Hartshorne hid his face in his hands as if he might make it all go away, as if he might uncover his eyes and see the hatchet gone and the fire gone and the storm cleared and the house filled again with wood and life. He could not help but hear the fire crackle musically. Ruby light stretched strange masques and arabesques across walls and ceiling. The snow piled up, higher and higher, and soon reached his shoulders, and still Hartshorne did not move. He was blind, surrendered, numb. The snow froze him deep, and stopped his trembling, and kept on piling up, up, up, now to his chest, his shoulders, his neck. . . .

Heather said she thought it was time to leave.

CHAPTER 25

TREMOR

They departed for Devonshire the next morning.

They took a coach as far as they could. When Heather recognized the landscape, she sniffed the air significantly, then shouted up to the coachman to let them out in what appeared to him to be the middle of nowhere. The coachman did so with an air of perplexity, and not without a great volley of questions regarding the safety, sanity, and wisdom of such a two as they, traipsing off into a forsaken moor with no means to find their way back to civilized company. Did they know, for instance, that the nearest town was no less than forty miles away? Or that this stretch of moor was known to be prowled by wolves? Or that, only days ago, on this stretch of road, the notorious highwayman Isambard Smyte had held up a duchess on her way to Cornwall, and robbed her of jewels and other valuables worth something in excess of twenty thousand pounds? Did they realize that in leaving his coach, they exposed themselves to these and many other dangers? Indeed, what did they mean by it? Foolishness! He would not hear of it!

In fact, it took some convincing to dismiss him, and to assure him that they would be safe, and that they did in fact have a place to go which was very nearby, though for their own reasons they could not name it.

The coach rattled off toward Cornwall as dusk began to settle. Heather lit a lantern.

They walked together on the moor, one lantern between them, lighting their way through heather and peat. The moor beyond the lantern's glow seemed to fall away into nothing, as though they were still traversing their way through Hartshorne's black tunnels. Only the occasional hoot of an owl reminded them that the moor spread out farther than they could see, and soon even these sounds seemed to dwindle away.

Milton felt very small. The breath of Hartshorne's winter still chilled him. Walking next to Heather, he felt that if he mirrored her footsteps, he could fend off the snowflakes with her presence and the warmth of the lantern, and leave that winter behind. But he knew that if he stood still, the flakes would begin to powder his hair, his coat, his hands.

He kept walking.

They hardly spoke. And yet, there was something immensely comforting about that globe of light, and their footsteps treading within it. It became a sort of sanctuary from the rude howls of Hartshorne's storm, muffling them away, and the hazel gleam in Heather's eye as she probed the night for landmarks, and her mild delight as the journey whetted her appetite for adventure, comforted Milton beyond measure. It was as though the peace of Tillington Road lived between them, and as long as the lantern kept shining, they could walk forever in that protective place, leaving Hartshorne, highwaymen, and hostile moor behind.

Yet he dared not draw too close, because Milton still did not know what to make of Heather. He was torn between two opposing views. On the one hand, he suspected that she had been to Larking Land, which gave her an air of heightened mystery; while on the other, she was far too daring in everything she did to be safe. This dual perception finally came to a head when Heather broke the silence with some idle talk, to help distract them and pass the time.

It started with a conversation about figs.

Heather said she liked figs. Milton said he didn't. Heather asked specifically *what* he didn't like about them, and Milton couldn't say, really, except he knew he didn't like them. Upon quizzing him further she learned that he really only ate four foods: sweetmeats, potatoes, shepherd's pie, and muffins.

(Five, if you count the occasional blancmange, but that was a treat.)

Curious.

Next, she learned that his idea of a night out "on the town" consisted of a solitary stroll down Tillington Road or, if he wanted to really do it up, a visit to Madame Tussaud's Waxworks. The same street, the same museum, every time.

Curious.

When she asked how someone could possibly go back to the same display week after week and still enjoy it, the question didn't make sense to him. How could someone *not* enjoy it, week after week?

All this led to a great many other discoveries about Milton that were all decidedly strange. Why, if he was a collector, did he never sell any of his paintings? Why hadn't his avocation led him to travel before this? Perhaps the most curious thing of all was that none of these things struck Milton as being curious. The only thing about their conversation that struck him as the least bit odd was the fact that Heather was asking so many personal questions.

"Why do you want the statue so badly?" she asked.

He suddenly became distracted, and muttered something about how he didn't know why, he just wanted it.

"You must know," said Heather. "People don't run all over the country looking for something without knowing why they want it."

With some reservation, Milton explained how beautiful the statue was, or must be, judging by the sketches in the notebook, and that he wanted to see the sculpture in person. His eyes kept darting about like frightened fish in two bowls.

As they spoke, Milton noticed a thin layer of mist creeping along the ground, settling up ahead.

Heather looked dubious. "You would really go to all this trouble for one statue just because you liked the sketches?"

They had reached the mist now, a patchy, shifting blanket of fog that thickened by the minute. The farther they walked, the thicker it became. Now it became opaque in places. Milton saw his shoes disappear, then reappear beneath him.

"What are you going to do with it, once you find it?" Heather asked.

Milton stammered that he would take it back to his museum.

"A great deal of trouble for one statue."

Milton heard a deep rumble shiver through his frame. Heather didn't seem to notice. At the same time, he felt a strong draft, saw it stir the fog, and felt fine dust tickle his throat.

Heather's eye met his, sly, birdlike.

"What's the *real* reason you want the statue?"

Rumble.

She smiled, bemused, waiting for his answer.

He did not smile back.

All around them, fissures were opening up in the ground. Plumes of dust spouted from the cracks as they growled open, widened into chasms, and breathed up frosty winds. They ate away more and more ground until the moor closely resembled fjords, with Milton and Heather toeing their way across the slender fingers of land reaching out above a cold ocean of darkness.

"I mean, you must have some special reason to go to so much trouble for a work of art you've never seen."

"I like Larking's work!" Milton barked. "That's all."

"But I thought you said you don't have any in your collection."

"I said I don't have any *on display*. I had one."

"What did you do with it?"

Rumble!

Milton staggered, froze in his tracks. The ground broke up all around him. Through the patchy fog he could now see only a scattering of islands hovering above a dark void. He looked directly below him. He stood on the edge of a small fragment of stone. The lantern light cast down into the blackness, but found nothing—at first. He stood paralyzed, vertigo swimming in his head, and then he saw it, far, far down. Something lashed, craned a barbed head. Leathery wings fanned the darkness. . . .

The birdlike eye blinked.

Milton swallowed, hard.

The smell of brimstone burned his nostrils as he tried to speak. "I kept it . . . tucked away."

"What do you mean, 'tucked away'?"

The rumbling subsided. The islands began to drift, stone lily pads on an invisible pond.

Apparently, Heather had no idea what was happening. She walked idly from one island to the next with the same nonchalance in her stride as before, without a glance at the ground, or any indication that she had a notion that the moor was falling away beneath them. Milton wanted to warn her to watch her step, but he noticed the most uncanny thing: though she never looked down, she just happened to step in the right place every time. If her stride lengthened, it did so just as the islands happened to be spaced farther apart.

Then she drifted away from him, and she came so dangerously close to slipping off that Milton's stomach clenched as her toe balanced on land while her heel balanced on air. His throat caught until she stepped to the next island's center, safe—for the moment. But she never even flinched.

He remembered reading about sleepwalkers who could safely traverse nocturnal landscapes by nothing more than the light of the moon, completely surefooted, yet all the while wholly unaware of their surroundings. It struck him that Heather behaved in exactly the same way, and he feared what might happen if he rippled the pool of her blissful ignorance by waking her to the danger beneath her.

If you wake a sleepwalker, they say it will make them go mad. In Heather's case, it might cause her to fall.

He didn't say anything. He just kept watching the ground, walking gingerly, the mossy stones giving him brief respite, the slick ones sending his heart racing.

Though she didn't notice that she was walking on the Edge of the World, she did notice Milton's odd behavior. Milton had stammered something about what he meant by "tucked away," about how it was rather difficult to explain, really, quite difficult to put into words exactly what he meant. No, no, it was impossible, positively impossible. Too esoteric. Rather vexing, actually, not to be able to explain it, but he simply couldn't.

Heather abandoned her line of inquiry, and returned to his side. Her birdlike eye studied him, and it was so close, but Milton could not meet it. Her lips parted as though she had more to say, but Milton hid in his frock coat, his mouth clamped tight.

They walked awhile in silence, Heather looking into the darkness ahead, Milton staring at his feet.

She didn't ask any more questions.

Eventually, the mists began to clear.

Soon only thin vapors, then nothing. When the fog lifted, the ground was restored, solid.

CHAPTER 26

REBELLIONS

"According to the journal, the pavilion should be somewhere in those hills to the north, just on the other side of this moor, over there." Adrian's human bloodhound pointed to a lushness not more than a day beyond their reach.

"Are you sure?" Adrian asked.

"As sure as I can be, based on the clues in the journal. We'll soon find out whether it was worth the price you paid."

Adrian's horse fretted. He reined him in hard. He squinted at the hills beyond the moor.

Another of his men: "Mr. Plackett, you promised to let us break for a bite before dusk. Well, it's nearly dusk now, and this place seems as good as any—"

"We can't stop now," said Adrian. "We're too close."

Another member of the hunt: "Betsy needs a rest," he said, patting the sweaty neck of his horse. "You can bargain with men, Mr. Plackett, but not with beasts. When Betsy needs to rest, by George, she'll rest, and that's all there is to it." Betsy duly showed protest by slowing and resisting any attempts to goad her on.

"Not yet. Do you see those hills? That's where the pavilion lies. We can reach it by dawn if we keep a steady pace all night."

"What? That's madness!"

"Keep moving!" Adrian scowled his heckler down. Whipping his steed, he led the way.

He pulled a few paces in front of the rest, distancing himself from their complaints.

The world is full of rebellion, thought Adrian to himself. Wasn't that the way the whole trip had been? One long rebellion, from beginning to end. Nothing would cooperate. The equipment balked, shifting in the trunks and unbalancing their loads; and the men repacked them so that they would shift again, almost as if they planned it as an excuse to stop the expedition, so they could slip in extra meals and needless rests. The horses revolted. One would spook at a hornet, or the sound of wolves at night. Another would throw a shoe. They all ate far too much, sometimes snatching mouthfuls of grass as they rode, so that he had to rein them up hard and scold them, the gluttonous brutes. His clothing fidgeted. His cufflinks, his waistcoat, his boots, none of them would sit straight on him, or cooperate with him. Even now, his ascot refused to stay straight about his neck. He tugged at it irritably. Not now, you filthy thing, not now!

In his efforts to stamp out rebellions, he had run himself nearly to exhaustion, but found his last fit of strength burning in him as the far hills promised to put an end to his pursuit.

He could not stop now.

Whenever the fever of the chase boiled in his veins, there was no stopping, only a ruthless headlong rush toward his quarry, so very nearly bagged, so close he could smell it. This had been his longest hunt, and this, he knew, his greatest quarry. If he could only catch it, if he could only catch it . . .

He had chased so many others, and all of them had glittered, and all of them had promised, and each had filled him with the same boiling fervor, yet after capture each one had in some little way betrayed him. They would go up on the wall, and he would show them off to his colleagues, but it would not be long before the rebellions would begin. Crooked. Dusty. Poorly lit. This one was not in as good a condition as he had thought when he purchased it. And that one there—what's this? Was he mistaken, or had it faded in the sunlight? Wasn't it duller than before?

Down to the basement.

Some merely lost his interest, a jester who told the same jokes. King Adrian was not amused. To the dungeon, you!

He whipped his horse again, dug his heels into its ribs.

A caravan of protests followed.

Even after the night caused his party to fall behind, he kept going, and did not take his eyes off that point to the north where the pavilion lay waiting somewhere in the hills of Devonshire.

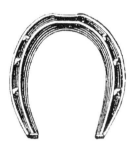

CHAPTER 27

SANCTUARY

Today I could swear this field is as wide as the whole world. I could walk in any direction all day, and never reach the end. I walk every day, and it seems I can hardly take two steps before I discover something new. Is there any end to it? I think it goes on like this forever. . . .

—LARKING'S JOURNAL

She could recognize the symptoms in an instant. Stomach-butterflies. No doubt about it.

How many times had she seen it? In more ballerinas and prima donnas than she could count. The butterflies set their feet pacing, set their fingers to tugging at their costumes or fussing about their hair, clipped their conversation into monosyllables. She could read the fine pinches of backstage faces and know who was nearing their cue. By the look of Milton, he was reaching his.

Ever since the conversation that had panicked him, Milton had shrunken back to his mouselike stature and scurried along, his pinkish nose sniffing admonitions. When they topped the brow of a hill, Heather pointed and said, "We're here." This is when the butterflies visited Milton.

It dawned on her then that Milton had always had a look of anticipation, only now it came into sharper focus, as though this scene he was about to play had been rehearsed for years. What scene it was, and how he would play it out, Heather could only guess. But she could never watch a victim of the butterflies without feeling a twitter of them herself. She felt them now.

Who was this strange little man?

He was someone who stammered and talked to his shoes or sometimes to some imaginary point very far away, someone who squinted, blinked, and held his hands up to shield his eyes whenever the spotlight turned on him. Someone who would rather wrap himself in gaslit fog than milling crowds, who sipped those night silences like vintage port, relished them like an invisible banquet. A man who forgot clocks and puttered in a world as small as a thimble, but who found more space and freedom and richness in that miniature country than most find in the most grandiose travels. Someone who conversed with wax-men and glided gondola-smooth down night streets, parting the darkness and pulling forth its hidden secrets like a magician dredging up rabbits, pigeons, doves.

In short, the strange little man named Milton Radcliffe was someone with one foot in one world and the other someplace else, and she wanted to know on what mysterious ground that other foot rested.

A child. A ghost. A still-life, rendered in oils. That was Milton.

Heather never could resist puzzles.

She almost called out to him, but she knew better than to break the concentration of someone preparing to go onstage. She waited in the wings, and watched.

It would all be just as he had imagined, wouldn't it?

Hadn't Heather described it? And didn't her description fit his picture of what Larking Land should be?

Yes, yes. He could hear her tell it now: The wild play of wine bottles and cherry smoke and Larking's lively brush, wine-dark-stained to capture the poppies in their gossip, a calico blanket and a wicker basket, and Heather among it all, capering.

Now, here they were. He could see the pavilion from here.

A breeze hissed through the oats, rose and fell, rose and fell. When he listened carefully, he could hear voices mingled in, whispering.

Come close, come close.

Down through the mint patch, down through the bed of bluebells . . .

The bluebells did not speak. They held their silver tongues.

He found a pond hidden in a basin canopied by a copse of birches. The water was still as rock, as though some giant had poured liquid jade into the water and let it harden there. Milton searched the depth of the pond, but found only a geometry of branch-shadows reaching through the stone.

Down through the cotton grass, down through the switchbacks, down through twitching cattails . . .

The field was flecked with dockweeds sprouted up all around him, all bent in the same direction, rusty fingers pointing toward a gabled roof not a stone's throw away.

The dockweeds pointed, and Milton followed, down a slope he had dreamt of, or forgotten, or . . .

Meadow smells.

He drank them in, a spicy wine of jasmine and yarrow and things he could not name, but knew. He drank them in long draughts, and remembered.

Every fiber in him trembled.

There—the door.

A little walk of weathered stones led to a large cottage. A slate roof and three gables rose out of ivy which encroached up the walls. A single chimney sent up no smoke. The door stood open, and might have stood that way for years.

He crossed the threshold.

A scattering of moldy straw covered the floor. Patches of mildew mottled the walls, and the air smelled as though nothing had moved through it in a century. Slates had fallen off the roof, revealing patches of sky through holes in the ceiling, an overcast that looked as though it suppressed within its fathoms the heart of a storm that, for the moment, held its peace. A patient, diffuse glow shone through the holes, and nothing more.

He crossed one threshold after another, going from room to room, each time as though he had opened the curtain on a play without actors. He tiptoed through each stage, careful not to disturb any articles left behind in case the actors might return any minute to reclaim them. Perhaps they stood invisibly in the room even now. He attended each prop and artifact with a care he had practiced for many years.

Softly, softly.

He never found more than two chairs in any room. In one, he found two seats opposite each other at an intimate little table. A single cupboard housed two plates, two cups, and two bowls, all earthenware unmistakably fashioned by Jonathan Larking himself, and in a drawer beneath it, handcrafted cutlery. Somehow, the clever craftsman had kiln-fired oaks into the bowls. He saw their knobby faces looking back at him. And the cups? One could not plunge a spoon into them without striking up whirlpools in an Earl Grey sea, and sending up gull-clouds in noisy flocks. The plates? As he looked carefully beneath the glaze, Milton found the meadow he had traversed outside, with something added: salad-tossed amid the phlox and yarrows, there were the footprints of dozens upon dozens of walks overprinting each other in countless trails. Despite the layers all crisscrossing each other, he could read the nature of the walkers' conversation by the way the footprints fell. Here they bounded—Jonathan raving to Lorien about a deer he saw that morning, red as a rose. Here they staggered to and fro—Jonathan clutching at the air, telling of a probing talk between himself and a friend that had spiraled to staggering heights and led them to a blinding summit where they both stood, white-lit and revealed. Here Larking pondering a mystery, and there revealing a silly notion that had once sent him round in circles but now only made him laugh; and here Larking bringing out a great miscellany of

conversation-trinkets that needed to be talked about, all the little gems too easily missed, but saved, from eulogies to buttered peas to boyhood marble-game victories relived, pocketfuls of stories he had forgotten until he began to dig them out. And *here* (the footprints grew very close), Jonathan listening, and Lorien telling *her* tale—of what, Milton could not decipher, but it was told in a hush, not because any eavesdropper had a chance of hearing, but because it was that kind of story.

It dawned on Milton that such plates had the special purpose of flavoring the food upon them with all the confessions glazed within them. A sliver of pie set upon one would soak up all the tales, and the person who ate that pie, having filled himself not only with rhubarb but with all the little secrets, would no doubt let slip a few of his own, until a dessert for the stomach progressed to one of shared confidences, and lips smacked not from sugared crusts but sugared tales served up well into the night.

He found no clocks within the pavilion. Why need there be any clocks here? The rooster crowed, and up sprang Jonathan to whip up his linseed swamp and rush toward the canvas wall to capture the unseen day. The sun begins to melt on the horizon? Jonathan leaps through fireflies and cotton grass, swaps a smock for a smoking jacket, kindles a fire, lands like Nellerelium on Queen Lorien's scepter, and gives his fresh report of all he's seen. The days could go on like that without hours or numbers, and no doubt they did. Jonathan honed his vision, tiptoeing through damp fern-lands by day, galloping over stark moon-hills by night, chasing comet-tails and moths, snapping the shutter of his mind's eye to bring home fresh visions and re-create them with his brush, or with his words and hands, smearing wild murals on the air in bold gestures as he told his wife of all he saw.

Such was the drama teeming within the bowls and plates. Although it awoke something within Milton, it was a drama in which he played no part. He must keep searching.

In the next room, an easel, a palette, a brush, a blank canvas stretched years ago and now sagging like the head of a tired drum.

On a little table next to it, a corncob pipe.

In the corner, a giant paper eye.

A breeze animated the eye in a blind wandering, its brittle paper shivering.

The eye looked at Milton.

Milton retreated from its sightless gaze, down a narrow hall that opened onto a spacious central room—a gallery. A single word was carved in the archway above its entrance:

SANCTUARY

There, on a pedestal in the center of the room, stood Lorien.

The walls of the chamber dissolved away to reveal rolling lavender hills stained in brooding cloudlight that had just begun to darken into dusk. Beyond Lorien, down a grassy slope, he saw his own Radcliffe House, no windows lit, dark within, curtains ghost-fluttering lazily through open windows.

Lorien awoke. Without a word, she stepped from her pedestal, looked at Milton as if inviting him to follow, walked toward Radcliffe House, and disappeared inside. Milton followed her in.

He glided amid the sleeping tomes and vases. The venerable oaken face atop the foyer mirror lifted a groggy eyelid, revealing a cloudy eye. It held a finger to its lips, begging silence. Beyond him, nothing moved or breathed. The floor was carpeted in dust, and his every footstep printed a cloud upon the air. The furniture, too, was coated with dust, and the chandeliers were draped in cobwebs. Though he had lost sight of Lorien, she had parted her way through the cobweb-curtains and left footprints in the dust carpet which Milton passed through his den, past a familiar teacup, now tired and cracked, past a familiar reading chair, now sagged and broken. He looked in the teacup briefly. A spider had made a home of it. A cup of webs.

The footprints continued next to the secret panel. He slid the panel and entered the secret gallery to discover that it had been restored to its pristine condition just as it had been before the fire, with two exceptions: first, it was empty; and second, the far wall was missing.

The footprints led toward the missing wall, and disappeared into an opaque curtain of mist.

Milton walked to the edge of the room where the wall should have been and reached into the mist gingerly with one foot, testing for solid ground. When he found it, he took a step, and then another, and when he soon found himself enveloped in the mist, he could taste the moisture of it and feel its dampness clinging to him. The curtain closed behind him, swallowing the gallery with it, leaving him with only the dew smell and a vast white haze, and veiled view of the ground. It was as though he were a giant looking down from his lofty vantage point at glimpses of the Earth as it shows itself through cloud formations that roll over its surface. He began to suspect that he really had grown to the stature of a giant, until he emerged from the mist in a land he had seen before, which once again shrank him to human size.

A moor all waste and blood-red earth.

The last stretch of land before World's End.

The ground stank of sulfur where it had been scorched; and where it hadn't been scorched, the blood-red earth gave way to a fine gravel of bones that crunched beneath his tread. The sea of mist had retreated, but not completely. He could see the moorland plain extending for miles in every direction, but always it ended with neither landmark nor horizon to give him any bearing. Reasoning that a walk in any single direction would ensure that he would not retrace his steps, he plodded forward to the steady beat of his own footsteps, without any notion where forward led or, even if he had known, what he would find there.

He marched until he ached.

The hypnosis of his footsteps carried him farther than he ever thought he could walk.

He stopped.

He had found the End of the World.

It had come upon him so suddenly, his mindless march might have carried him right over the Edge. No horizon announced it, no signposts delineated it. The world just fell away sheer-faced to misty infinity, a single glance at which had sent him reeling in dizzy retreat.

He tossed a stone.

It made no sound.

The mist here more closely resembled clouds, and upon closer scrutiny he thought he could see things tucked away in their formations. Squint as he might, he could not improve his vision. He was ready to give up when he found a brass cylinder at his feet.

A telescope.

He swept the view with the instrument, probing the mist beyond World's End. A mile or two off, on a plane somewhat below him, he spied three islands. He examined each of them, one by one.

On the first island was a single mountain, and at the top of the mountain, a single cave. Milton pointed the telescope at the mouth of the cave, and adjusted it until he could see inside, so clearly and so closely that it was as if he actually stood on the very lip of the cave, looking in. The opening of the cave was tremendous, the inside, very dark.

There was, however, a little puddle of light surrounding a wooden desk. Candles fortified the desk's perimeter like a small castle wall, and their drippings spilled from desktop to floor in petrified rivers. Beyond the illumination afforded by the candles, the rest of the cave danced in long shadows, but Milton could make out two details: a littering of snapped lances on the floor and a pile of bones.

Here, seated at the desk, hunched Thulemander, very much at home, working quietly.

What better place to pen his tales? And more to the point, what better place to cull them?

Such was the kind of person that Thulemander was.

The kind to bargain with Dragons. Yes.

Whenever a Dragon came to Thulemander, *he* did not cower beneath the covers in his bed.

He took notes. Dictation.

The Dragon told him all he knew of World's End, and he recorded every syllable, and that is how he came to know the history of the Sea of Darkness and those creatures that spawned from within it.

What kind of deal the cartographer had made, and why a Dragon chose not only to spare Thulemander but to indulge him, Milton could not guess. Nor could he guess how Thulemander survived in the Dragon's lair. Whereas most would have choked on the cave's poisonous air, Thulemander inhaled it like a tonic.

Some will sip bitter wines, and call them sweet. Thulemander was a lightning rod baiting chaos to strike, and when it struck, Thulemander crackled.

The Dragon had hissed its history and said that it was so, and Thulemander charted it thusly, and had made it so in his notes and in his sketches, tracing out all the implications of the lecture to their logical extremes. Charting plagues, indexing conspiracies, and cataloging the demise of the civilized world, Thulemander, fueled by the intelligence of the forked tongue that had come to him in the night, had crafted his *Cosmographie* in exquisite detail.

So the Dragon came and the Dragon went, and Thulemander stuck to his scholarly post in a sunless academy divorced from the civilized world, diligently writing in a perpetual dungeon twilight. The only indication of his never-ending sacrifice were the circles under his eyes (which, lacking a mirror, he never saw). No human contact interrupted the flow of his calculations, which filled page after page after page after page. . . .

Milton turned the telescope toward the second island.

It was far below him, so that as he looked down at it he could see the whole configuration of its landscape. It was very small, treeless, with a hard-packed soil that gave off a muddy glimmer. Again he adjusted the telescope to move in closely, and again it was as though he now stood upon the island, or this time, as though he hovered directly above it. He first mistook a series of channels for a hedge-maze, but realized that these were actually trenches carved deep into the earth. As he adjusted the telescope's focus more tightly, he saw that a few paintings were scattered throughout, not hung but propped against walls here and there, as though abandoned. Besides that, the maze of trenches was empty.

No—no, not quite. A single figure rounded a corner and came into view.

Adrian Plackett, in fine form, was pursing the Crown Jewel for his Collection, all in the name of preserving the harmony of the Diorama. He never looked up, he never looked to either side. His vision was locked on a course dead ahead, and his cane was at the ready, so as to bat aside anything that might get in his way.

From his vantage point, Milton could see that a very beautiful painting lay within the collector's path. Adrian huffed and bellowed. Milton followed his progress. Adrian turned the corner of the maze, the painting came into his line of sight, he headed straight for it, produced a measuring tape, measured it, scrutinized it with an opaque look which wilted into disgust, tossed it aside, marched onward.

Round and round the corners he went.

At another painting, the same process ensued: measure, scrutinize, look of disgust, toss aside, march onward. Milton watched several repetitions of this routine. At one juncture, Adrian retraced a path he had traversed earlier, and trampled one of the paintings he had tossed aside.

The frame crunched beneath his foot.

Milton thought of the hard-packed mud that glimmered a dirty gold.

Could it be?

Milton focused on a wall within the maze. It was composed of a strange stratum that looked curiously similar to an artist's palette. The layers of colors resembled the sludge of mixed paints, flecked throughout with wood and gold leaf.

How long would it take to toss so many paintings aside, trample them underfoot, compress them into a sediment of oiled canvas and linseed frame, and pace and pace and pace until you had worn grooves down through it all, and created your own maze?

When Milton focused very tightly on Adrian, he could see that the collector's face glistened with sweat. Somehow, Milton knew that this was not sweat brought about by exertion. It was the sweat of a fever. His snowy ascot wilted, his hands lightly trembled as he gripped each frame the way a convict might wring the bars of his prison cell, and his hands, too, were moist with sweat. A fire that gave no flash of flame or billow of smoke, but only smoldered deep at his core, consumed him from within, and no amount of pacing would snuff the thing out.

The figure turned a corner, and was gone.

Adrian, in his own labyrinth, was himself both victim and Minotaur, in a hunt that would not end.

Milton turned his telescope to the third island, the smallest of them all.

It was covered with snow stained with ash. In the middle of the island, a forest all charred and sooty sent up tendrils of smoke, and glowed here and there with eyes of amber.

In the middle of the forest, a little man was digging through the snow and ashes, looking for something. All around him, the forest muttered, crackled.

The snow powdered his hair, his coat. His cheeks were stung red with frost, and his breath plumed the air evenly as he searched the snow bed with his hands. He dug in one place, found nothing, stood up, studied the snow as if he might be able to see through it or read its gentle slopes, and discern what he might find beneath. He resumed his search as one who has begun a long day's work that he expects to be very hard, but greets with patience. He knelt in the snow, scooping it gently.

Nearby, a smoking trunk groaned, shifted. It was too nearby for the man not to hear it, yet he did not turn around.

The trunk cracked.

It fell, and nearly hit him.

He did not even flinch. The dead trunk lay hissing in the snow next to him in a rush of steam and swirl of ash that resembled a great gray ghost.

He continued with his work.

Milton recognized the face. A hundred questions raced to mind.

(After that night when your Enchanted Forest burnt down, why didn't you pick up your carving tools and get to work again? When did you lose those tools, and where?)

Softly, one scoop, and then another. Unstained. Pure.

Another tree fell.

Another ghost rose.

(After that night when you fed the forest into the fire, who did you tell? Anyone?)

His hands were two fragile birds, fluttering.

Another ghost rose, and mouthed the words: *You're lost.*

Mr. Hartshorne dug in the snow. He did not look up, he did not speak to the trees about what they were doing to him. Each creak and splinter only fueled his work, upon which he was completely set, and out of which nothing could summon him.

(Will you find your carving tools there, and if you do, will your hands remember them? When did the tools slip from your hands, Mr. Hartshorne? They must be here somewhere. Where did you leave them?)

Another tree fell. No matter. Keep digging. The snow was soft and weightless, a balm that numbed his fingers, quieted those fragile birds, eased them to sleep.

You're lost.

(Will you find the Golden Child in there, and if you explained it all to him again, do you think he would understand this time? Would that stop the trees from falling?)

Dig, little birds. Scratch the ground.

The ghost undulated hypnotically.

Dig, Mr. Hartshorne.

One scoop, and then another. Pure. Light as air.

The snow settled on him, powdered his hair, his coat.

Another tree fell. Something cracked in Mr. Hartshorne's face. His digging became a little meaner.

They must be here, somewhere.

Dig faster, Mr. Hartshorne.

(Perhaps you think that if you dig deep enough, you will find more than just your tools? Perhaps you think you can exhume the Enchanted Forest, piece by piece, and all the mystery and laughter that filled it, if you just keep digging? Will you find little Heather sleep-shrouded in the snow, and will she remember where you let the tools slip from your hands?)

You're lost.

Just keep digging.

(Will she play this game of pick-up sticks with you? It's child's play, isn't it?)

Behind him, all around him, ghosts swayed. One mouthed a parting word before twisting up into the fog: *Lost.*

Hartshorne dug deeper, losing his patience, but he refused to surrender. Milton knew he would never give in. He would dig until his hands were blue. He would dig and dig, to the end of time.

Milton lowered the telescope and looked out at the three distant islands with his naked eye. So far away, he thought. Had he shouted to any of them, they would not have heard him, not merely because they were out of earshot. Thulemander in the Dragon's lair, Adrian in his labyrinth, Hartshorne in his forest—all were inaccessible. Each had created a personal exile that was impenetrable. He could have stood on each island's shore and shouted for all he was worth. They would not have heard.

Milton ran a million miles back toward Radcliffe House, but the house was gone.

In its place Madame Tussaud's Waxworks loomed up much taller than he had remembered it, and tilted. Upon entering, he found a high Gothic corridor inside that stretched as far as he could see, with no door in sight, nor any inhabitants. His footsteps tumbled up into the vast ceiling, and echoed long after he stood still.

Scritch.

A scratching sound echoed back from farther down the hall.

Milton traced the sound to a doorway which led into a tremendous studio wherein a single figure sat, a woman in a musty midnight dress. She worked at a well-lit table among a clutter of tools, her back to the door, so that she did not see Milton enter, and was evidently too absorbed in her work to take notice of him. As he stepped closer, he heard the *scritch, scritch, scritch* of her tools as she carved away at something, and he could see now that her coif of dark hair was streaked with threads of gray. The dress might have been salvaged from some limned moorland ruin.

He stepped still nearer. She did not react.

As he watched over her shoulder, he could see her aged but nimble hands working a pick as she put the finishing touches on a wax head. He could see the faintest line of talc that stopped where her jaw ended and her neck began, the faintest delineation of a mask.

She turned the head over. Milton gasped when he recognized who it was.

Mr. Hartshorne.

The woman did not look up from her work. She plucked at the head with her tools. Shavings of wax fell to the floor in delicate curls.

"I'll be ready for you in just a moment," she said without turning around.

Milton was at a loss for words.

"You may get ready if you like." She indicated a stool situated favorably in the light. When Milton failed to take up her offer, she only continued with her work on Hartshorne's head.

"I think I've made a mistake," said Milton.

(Scritch, scritch.)

"I've come in here by accident. I'm sorry to have disturbed you." He began to bow out.

(*Scritch, scritch, scritch.*) "You visit my museum every week for nearly ten years, and now you say you came in here by accident?"

Her museum. Yes.

"That's not what I mean. I mean, I don't know why I came here."

Madame Tussaud set down her tools and turned to regard her guest. Her cheeks were neatly rouged, so subtly, he might not have detected the makeup had he not looked for it, and her eyes were lined spider-thin with eyeliner. A stately face. But didn't it resemble a little too closely the handiwork he had seen in her museum?

Whatever the rest of Madame Tussaud was made of, her eyes were not made of glass. They looked too deeply into him, and saw too much. Yet she was not concerned with what she saw. Like a doctor who has seen sickness too many times to react with pity or repugnance, she eyed him squarely and coolly only for a moment, then brushed the wax from her hands as she stood.

"Why did you visit the museum for all those years?"

Milton said he didn't know.

"You visited a place every week for nearly ten years without knowing why?"

Milton had no answer.

"Here. I'll show you why."

The pool of light expanded to reveal three wax figures, one of which was missing its head.

The headless one was Mr. Hartshorne, whose shoulders were dusted with snow.

The second figure was a precise replica of Adrian Plackett, who brandished his cane in one hand, his ledger in the other. Framed in snowy cravat and freshly steamed top hat, the face—not real? Too real. As Milton studied the hard-set eyes he could hear the Ringmaster shouting again, "Crooked! You call that straight? It's crooked! Crooked!"

Behind him, Milton could see the backdrop for this figure's display under construction. Madame Tussaud had begun to erect walls, mimicking in papier-mâché what had taken Adrian years to create from the spoils of his collection: the Maze.

Beneath the third figure, a little plaque read: THULEMANDER OF WESSEX.

The scowl of his caterpillar eyebrows, the roundness of his shoulders as he hunched over his book, the circles under his eyes, deeper than ever—she had captured it all faithfully. A worm-pale hand crawled over a tattered page of the *Cosmographie*. Behind him hung a disk like a tremendous gong. It was a map of Thulemander's World, all plagues, conspiracies, traps, and pitfalls pinpointed diligently thereon. Beyond it: Darkness.

Madame Tussaud fitted Mr. Hartshorne's head on. (It took a little jostling to get it straight.) She straightened his lapels and plucked out a stray thread or two, but she still did not find him presentable. She slapped him clean with a smart hand, and walked around him, inspecting until she was satisfied. There was something hideous about the way Mr. Hartshorne rocked when she swatted the snow off of him.

From out of the darkness she drew forth another figure, also complete except for the head. Milton recognized the body.

The posture was correct, the frock coat identical. From the mirror-bright shoes to the silk cravat ruthlessly straight, Madame Tussaud had captured him in perfect likeness. But she had stopped at the head. No head. Milton's double still waited for its head to arrive.

Madame Tussaud scrutinized Milton's face, examining every contour and line with a penetrating keenness. Her fingers twitched. She pointed again toward the stool, and asked him if he would not like to take his seat now, so she might begin?

On her worktable was a large, formless ball of clay with a few tools lanced into it.

She's trying to trap me, thought Milton.

Madame Tussaud studied him, and he studied Madame Tussaud, and behind her eyes he read her secret.

If she modeled you in wax, once the model was complete, you never could escape it. Once she had cast you and puttied you and painted you and propped you up in the cool recesses of her waxwork palace, you were like an insect caught in amber. Your real living was over, and whatever was left of you walking the streets outside was endlessly doomed to go through the motions of life in senseless repetition. The case in point was the trio that stood before him. She had embalmed each of them in a moment that defined them, and from which they would never rise.

"Let's begin, shall we?"

"No."

"What's the matter?"

Don't let her look at you, don't let her study your face. If she sees me too closely, she'll begin the sculpture, and I'll be trapped.

She folded supple waxen arms across her chest. "Well?"

"I'm sorry, but I didn't ask you to do this."

She arched a penciled eyebrow.

"I visited all those years, I know, and I don't know why I did, but I don't want to join the museum—"

Milton realized that she wasn't listening to him any more. She was studying his face. Her eyes shutter-blinked, clicked a photograph to her memory.

He turned and fled.

Radcliffe House was gone.

Once again, he was at World's End.

He searched the ravines and copses and valleys, but found no way back to the moor. Cliffs dropped on every side. He ran along the Edge until his lungs burned and his feet ached. He noticed another golden cylinder up ahead on the shore. He ran to it, picked it up.

It was the same telescope.

On the ground all around him were his own footprints in the sand, marking the place where he had started.

He had run a full circle.

He was trapped on an island.

Frost had stiffened the joints of the telescope, and blinded its lens. The brass was so cold it bit his fingertips.

No.

He hurled it over the Edge.

It disappeared into the fog.

Not a sound. No sound.

Milton wanted to hear the sound of it hit bottom, and when he didn't hear it, he grew angry.

"Lorien!"

He cried her name out in all directions. No answer.

"Lampyridae! Braymouth! Come on, everyone, where are you? I've come all this way."

The wind salted him with crystals of ice.

Milton scowled at the hazy oceans that boxed him in, defying their victory. The worst part was, there was no one to shake a fist at, or throw a rock at, no menacing snarl to glare back at in defiance. His conqueror wore no face, so gave his defiance no target. This conqueror grew denser and colder and gathered all its powers, and swallowed up the three islands in one torrential gust. Footprints? Any footprints? Lorien's footprints, anywhere?

He searched the ground for another telescope or some other tool or clue that might hint at a way of escape. He found only the hard, barren crust of empty plain, cracked and fissured like ancient mummy skin.

Milton was ready to shout how unfair it all was, how he felt cheated at having been led so far into a trap, how cruel it all was for his friends to abandon him when he had laid his whole trust in them. But despite the forlorn face of his surroundings, something told him this wasn't true.

He waited a long time. Nothing happened.

He stepped near the edge.

So this is it. This is the End of the World.

The gray wash and ebb of waves, vast and silent, invited him. Miles below, something whipped up tidepools that glided like mute tornadoes funneling emptiness. And somewhere, below the surface, a sulfuric growl rumbled through the sky like far lost thunder.

He stepped closer to the Edge, so close his toes touched the rim.

I can't stay here.

He closed his eyes, and spread his arms out in the same way he had seen Lampyridae do just before he rose weightlessly into the air.

I can't stay. I don't know why you brought me to this place, Lorien, but I can't stay. And I can't believe you would want me to stay in a place like this, so cold and lost and forgotten. I always ran to you to rescue me from places like this, and now I don't see anywhere else to run. If this is how it ends, then I don't understand, because it isn't like you. You've led me too far and done me too much good for me to believe that this is how it ends. I don't know what will happen, but then, it seems I never do anymore. It seems as though every time I try to figure things out, I'm wrong. I thought all I wanted was to find you again, and take you home to the gallery, but now I don't know if that's right. I don't know what to think. I don't know what will happen, but I'm going to trust you. I'm going to jump.

The wind rolled through the whiteness, and the gray. Eyes closed, he listened carefully. Did he hear the faintest sand-sift whisper? The softest birdlike voice, echoing a discouragement, an entreaty, a warning?

No. Only the rise and fall of the gusts, whirlwinds and fine sprays that pearled Milton's face, his hair, his fingertips. A single tear froze like a blue jewel on his cheek. He didn't move.

A single figure stood motionless on the shore of an island that floated in a sea of mist. Below him, a gray ocean, vast beyond measure, and bottomless, engulfed every horizon, every shore, and every landmark. It was a place where no foghorn blew, no semaphore flags waved, no foretopsman shouted from swaying crow's nest into the breeze, an ocean with neither buoy nor beacon to guide, where telescopes clouded, compasses spun in idiot circles, sextants pointed to nowhere. It was a sea of unknowns, an abyss of mystery, fathomless, faceless, unending.

The figure tipped gently, and dived like a swan, into the abyss. . . .

He fell and fell. Torrents blasted him, tossing him this way and that like a rag doll tumbling down through the funnel of a cyclone. He tumbled head over heels through riptides and hurricanes and layer upon layer of gray clouds, until storm gave way to fog and fog gave way to crisp midnight and he slid through a starry blue darkness, and felt himself slowing, as though he had gained a buoyancy, and finally descended through waters of night to touch down in a meadow that looked somehow vaguely familiar.

A night bird sang. Fireflies traced the air.

Somewhere, in some far-off vale, a donkey brayed.

A serene night in Larking Land.

In the distance, a mountain windmill.

In the dusky glow, its shingles glinted the same blue-gray sheen as the thistles themselves. The tremendous blades creaked a music that drew Milton near. He knew he had heard the music before, though he couldn't name it, and it guided him in a progression that his feet seemed to know already, although he could not explain where they had learned it. He walked up a cinnamon path until he faced the door at the base of the windmill. Overhead, an invisible stream rounded up the thistles and sluiced them down through the valley.

They whispered: *Welcome.*

An invitation. Brass knocker. Corn husk. The windmill door.

Milton stepped close. It opened of its own accord, and ushered him into a room that appeared to be waiting for him.

The old, cracked bellows. The crooked poker. The oak mantel clock atop the oaken mantel. He stood on a throw rug woven on a loom. He could tell by looking how it was made: the weaver had

scooped up wheat stalks and white corn kernels and chestnuts and pumpkins and blue-gray wren feathers and the silver gleam off sun-polished granite like the stones of the fence along Tillington Road, wadded them into a tremendous ball, spun them into threads with her spinning wheel, and woven them into a mosaic that braided them all together in twist-ings and turnings that seemed to have neither beginning nor end. To look at it was to walk down a meandering meadow trail in Larking Land, on the kind of walk that seems also to have neither beginning nor end.

He wiped his feet reverently.

The room was warm, the air heavy with scent: the burning birch log aglow in the fire-place, the spice ball hanging near the door, the steam from the berry pie cooling in the kitchen, a fragrance so tart his mouth began to water. The aromas wrapped around him, soft and snug.

On a sofa he found a ball of calico fur that he supposed to be a cat, curled into deep hibernation.

Milton removed his coat, and knew to hang it on the coat rack next to the entrance.

"This place is so familiar," he whispered to himself, careful to preserve a quiet he felt as deeply as the wind of Thistle River that had cleansed him moments ago.

The mantel clock ticked cheerfully to itself.

In the kitchen, the teapot began to simmer, a tiny thunderstorm brewing in a copper cave.

The ball of fur stirred, stretched, ungummed sleepy eyes, yawned.

He thought, I know that kettle. That mantel. That clock on the mantel. I've drunk from that mug, I've eaten off those plates. I know all of this, but from where?

No room in Radcliffe House had ever looked so much like home as this place, he knew that. Then where was he? And why did it feel so familiar?

He noticed along the wall a gallery of miniature photographs. They were each hardly larger than a postcard, yet each was framed in elegantly engraved gold, and given plenty of room on the wall, so that they drew Milton in. He searched every one, and recognized the scenes they depicted.

One: His coach ride toward Slackington, the essence of the countryside captured in a single view—the cottage, the row of haystacks, the farmer plowing his field.

Two: The shimmering palace that had risen when Heather sang her song. It shimmered there again, in miniature.

Three: The fireflies he had found in the wilderness that day, after he had told Heather about his snowy walk. The fireflies traced luminous doodles on the purple cloud-slate of an overcast sky.

Four: Nellerelium perched atop a reed, bowing an august bow.

Five: The bluebells laughing.

And on and on.

He seated himself in the wing-back chair, next to a side table, where he found his teacup, brimming with Earl Grey. Beside it was the sugar bowl, and a teaspoon.

Well, why not?

One, two.

The spoon chimed in the teacup cheerfully. Milton snuggled himself into his chair, and lost himself in its deeps, sighing with wonder.

"Where is this place?" he said aloud.

"It's home," a voice said behind him.

A woman in a cinnamon dress.

Heather.

He was so glad to see her, tears of joy rimmed his eyes.

He ran to embrace her, and he was no longer inside the windmill. He was outside the pavilion. He saw Heather on a grassy knoll in the distance, having a picnic lunch.

He ran to her.

CHAPTER 28

THE CONFESSION

He found Heather jumping up for a plum that dangled just above and beyond her grasp. Hop, hop! She nabbed it, polished it, bit into it luxuriously. Mmmm.

He told her everything. He told her about the secret gallery and the Larking painting and the fire and Thulemander and World's End. He told her about the Sea of Darkness, and the night the Dragon returned to his rooftop, and how it had followed him for years. He told her about Captain Tark and the chorus of screaming sailors he saw swimming in Thulemander's eyes. He told her about Lampyridae and Braymouth and the ships of Thistle Bay, and the long blue thread of Thistle River that wound up into the hills, and the real reason why it was so important for him to find the statue, and why he feels both confused and inexplicably at peace now that he's decided not to take Lorien back to Radcliffe House.

Heather listened very attentively, and never interrupted. When he was finished she waited quietly in case something more were to spill out of him. When she was convinced that he had finished (at least for the moment), she spoke softly, and very gently.

She said that Lampyridae seemed quite charming, and that Braymouth sounded like a wonderfully surly old fellow, and Thulemander absolutely dreadful; and that long cold falling over World's End was more terrifying than anything. She spoke of these things as though she might be half-familiar with them herself, as though she had visited the same country but not walked the same road.

Milton said that she must think him mad to come all the way out there and not take Lorien back with him.

Heather debated the question over another plum.

Her verdict: "Not at all. (My, this plum is sweet.)"

There was something in the way she said it that convinced him that she saw no problem at all in leaving Lorien right where they had found her. To her it seemed the natural thing to do.

The fact that someone else felt that way (who was clearly sane) meant everything to him. But he still didn't know why he had changed his mind. If he wasn't going to take Lorien home, why had he come all the way there?

Heather looked out at the slope of the meadow. "When I was a little girl and I stayed here that summer, Jonathan told me that this field is as big as the whole world. He was right, in a way." She studied a thistle or some other small thing in her hand.

Milton had been watching the sky too long. He closed his eyes to remedy the milky haze of too much cloudlight, and as he listened to Heather's description of a world-broad field, a memory from his trip dissolved into view like an old photograph, of the afternoon of his trundling toward Slackington in the coach. It all came back to him then. Clop of hooves. Jingle of bridle. A cottage. A row of haystacks. A farmer at his plow. The picture persisted, permanent, like the page of a book.

"Do you think the field is that big?" Heather asked.

(A tilted milestone. A yew tree, alone on an empty knoll.)

Milton said he didn't know.

Heather looked as though she expected some final shred of his tale to spill from him then, but he only looked down at his shoes, too exhausted to speak. He was wrung dry.

She gave him a hug.

Milton remembered a brief moment in a golden field when he was running forever.

Was it coming back piece by piece? Little pieces of what he had been looking for, all along?

Heather straightened his wrinkled coat, held out a purple jewel.

"Plum?"

CHAPTER 29

THE SECOND EXPEDITION
CONCLUDED

"There!"

A bloodhound pointed.

The pack circled their quarry.

The moment of the Crown Jewel was at hand. Adrian had rushed to claim the honor of being the first to cross the threshold, and was quite surprised to find that someone else had beaten him to it. The sight of fresh footprints leading into the cottage had nearly ignited him. Only after his men stormed the premises to lead him to the Sanctuary did he break his pace. Behold, Her Majesty.

He circled the statue, slowly.

One half of the party concentrated on the sculpture, the other half on Adrian.

The woman's feet were fused to the pedestal without seam, as if statue and base were both carved from a single stone.

The ebony cane twitched.

The pedestal, it seemed, was similarly attached to the stone floor, which was not assembled from a grid of individual flagstones as it should have been, but was instead a single slab, as though the floor of the cottage was the very bedrock of the site itself.

The ebony cane tested the floor to see if it was solid. Every inch of it. Others gathered without being able to find the trick. It was a trick, wasn't it? It couldn't be real. They all knew Larking was a genius, and they knew his reputation as an eccentric too well to ask what prompted such a construction, so they only probed the floor the way a boy might badger a prestidigitator, begging him to shuffle the shells around once more, and keep your hands in plain sight at all times, please!

Despite their persistence, Larking's device proved impenetrable. Either he had crossed some new frontier in geology and discovered a method to fuse rock, or else the pedestal really was carved from the floor, which really was bedrock.

The party called a recess to rally their resources, and their wits.

"Now how do you suppose he managed this?" Adrian put the question to his assembled team of experts.

Everyone spoke at once.

The Archeologist argued with his colleague, saying it wasn't possible. His colleague argued back, saying it *was* possible, but far too unlikely. The Art Historian assured them both that where Jonathan Larking was concerned, anything was likely. The decisive opinion proved to be that of the Geologist, who had made his living carving rock, and said that even though he had never heard of anything so ridiculous, he knew a solid piece of stone when he saw it, and there in the gallery, he saw it.

So, while the bloodhounds had cornered the statue, the academics themselves were cornered by brute fact, and searched about themselves for leverage. Several strategies were advanced, none of which made any sense—except one.

"He would have to carve the statue first, then build around it," someone suggested. "He must have built this whole cottage around this one statue. Isn't it incredible?"

Adrian parted his way through the quibbling men to retrieve the necessary tools. The one plan, the only possible plan that could take the Crown Jewel back, he would trust to no one but himself.

"One side!" said Adrian.

They all gaped at the instrument he held in his hand.

Tap, tap, tap.

In reading Jonathan Larking's journal, Adrian had come across a passage which spoke of the nature of stone. Larking said that every stone has hidden veins, hidden fissures. Although we see

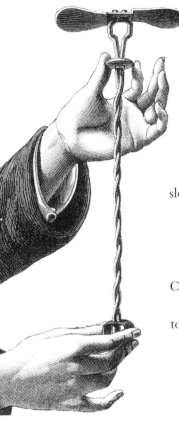

them as strong, in a very real way, all stones are very fragile. (Adrian had skimmed over this and forgotten it as soon as he had turned the page.)

Tap, tap, tap.

The bloodhounds froze.

An impatient chiseling sound continued for what seemed a year.

None of them had ever seen a stone split like that.

The two archeologists caught the statue as it fell.

"Is it all right?" asked the Geologist. "Let's have a look."

"Get away!" snapped Adrian.

The circle dissipated, all except the Geologist, who approached Adrian very slowly, the way a dog catcher might approach a rabid wolf.

"Here. Let me see."

"Crooked! It's crooked!"

"Not at all. You clipped it just right. A little sanding—"

"Get away from me! You think I can't see with my own eyes? It's crooked! CROOKED!"

It was a long trip back. Once the statue was packed and the coaches directed toward London, nobody spoke for the rest of the journey.

CHAPTER 30

LARKING LAND

In the days that followed, Milton could not help but wonder if he would find Heather there inside the windmill again, were he to return. Something told him that the windmill held many things, depending on who he was when he opened it, what he had become. What might he find next month, next summer, two, three, four long years from now? Would he find not a room but an open road leading out of London, beyond World's End, pointing him to some other expedition, somewhere? Would he find some relic he had lost from his childhood? A whirligig toy? A candle? A Jack-in-the-box? Or merely a Jack-in-the-box grin?

He might find the pages from the Book of Days flying loose in the funnel of a whirlwind, waiting for him to step in the middle and fly with them like Lampyridae up into the blustery night sky to toss like a tumbleweed over the purple hills. He might find two children turning skipping ropes and calling out his name, daring him to toss himself into their threshing mill like fool's hay. He might find Jonathan Larking in his circus-speckled smock, holding up a thumb to the landscape, photographing the invisible with his mind's eye, and wielding his brush with great dashes and strokes, smearing his canvas with life.

What might he find?

He might find Jacob Hartshorne half buried in his private winter, a confession frozen on his cold blue lips, waiting to thaw and trickle out his dark tale.

He might find Adrian Plackett blindfolded and collapsed in the wing-back chair out on Larking Meadow, a crumbled man, not chasing paintings any more, but finally searching for any hand that might reach out and deliver him from his self-made night.

What?

He could not say. What he *could* say was, he would find whatever he needed to find. Larking Land was everywhere now, in every spray of freckles on every bird's egg, in every cast of straw upon the floor, in every cartwheel and eddy of leaves, in the steam rising from the morning gables. The whole pavilion, which had seemed so sullen upon his arrival, was now charged with life. It was everywhere.

Milton wondered about something else: What had Heather found, on that day? What had she seen when she wandered off through the pavilion on her own? Had she found her own windmill, when she explored those rooms that contained whole worlds? And if she had, what did she find inside *her* windmill? he wondered.

Afterward, she had begun singing again—first humming, then purring, then growling, then roller-coaster soar-and-dipping through a whole menagerie of sounds before she finally returned to shaping melodies, cool and serene. What had she found?

Her voice, naturally.

Had it been tucked away in a walnut box upon a mantel, humming like a merry insect? Did she find it sealed tight in a Mason jar? Had it hardened into candy? She might simply have found it in the bottom of a drawer, squirreled away with other trinket-treasures long forgotten, now rediscovered: a locket, a thimble, a cat's whisker, a regal hair comb, a bracelet made of mother-of-pearl. She might have found it jangling in a little burlap sack filled with keys that had lost their locks. Or she might have found it in the biscuit jar. Who knows? There was no telling with her.

Heather sang.

And Milton, hard at work in another room, listened through the walls.

He mixed some pigments on a very old palette. Ochre. Magenta. A touch of yellow. Mingling the brush through it all in thoughtful strokes, he contemplated the splash of colors before him.

Heather had told him about her singing lessons. Her mother would say: "Lift your head. Lift your sternum. Lift your whole body by standing on your toes, and feel your weight poised and buoyant, as though you were ready to fly!"

Heather had told Milton her secret: When she sang, she imagined that her whole body was hovering in the air above the stage. Responding to her imagination, her posture would elevate itself. Her head lifted, her sternum rose high, and indeed she felt an exhilarating weightlessness that made singing easy.

Was it any wonder, then, that as Milton had watched her perform, she appeared as if she would, any moment, tumble up into the sky?

Had she ever been to Larking Land? Perhaps a better question was, had she ever really left it? Perhaps she didn't need to step through anything to go there. She had grown up steeped in Larking's linseed oils, surrounded by his meadows. Perhaps she always lived between one place and the other, singing onstage but seeing no audience, seeing instead a flock of smoke rings drifting up, forming lyrics, or riddles. Or perhaps she always carried a little piece of Larking Land tucked away in her luggage: a horseshoe from Braymouth, or a firefly in a jar.

He peered into the pigments, stirred them gently.

It's everywhere. I can see it.

He tickled the canvas.

Summer lightning spilled down the canvas wall.

The next day, the two of them on a long walk.

"It's everywhere, Heather. It's in the grass. It's in the trees. It's in the air."

She looked up into the lacework of branches above her and spun, and the leaves meshed into a wheel that whirled above her.

"My gosh, Heather, do you know where we are?"

She kept whirling, her arms out like a spangled circus lady dangling from a rope high above the ring. She pirouetted elegantly, faster and faster.

"Do you know?" he prodded.

Dazed, she stopped spinning, waited for the merry-go-round meadow to slow, slow, stop. When everything had settled and she took a good look around her, she knew the answer.

"In the Land of Bluebells," Heather said, very matter-of-fact.

"That's right!"

It was Larking's field, to be sure, and the seeds that had sprouted great paintings in his fertile mind were everywhere around them, crackling. Milton fell to a hushed awe, while Heather only hummed a few bars of some ditty under her breath. Maybe it was her own song, bubbling up from somewhere like a child's skipping-rope rhyme.

The tune worked its way through the briar wood and bramble, and worked its wonders. . . .

Something like blue fire leaped up in Milton's mind: a bed of bluebells.

A handful of fireflies spilled upward like dim stars fleeing up a chimney flue.

What could be said at a time like that? Everything that needed saying was written all over the countryside, in every direction: written large, across a blustery wash of clouds that wrapped the land in a hush, broken by the glossy dart of a single wren heading homeward; and written small, small, small, in the tiniest hollow of an acorn, or in the weathered flagstones of the path, or in a feather they found, a jettisoned oar blade, blue as summer. It was written everywhere, in every size in between. All that was left to do was to walk a lazy, wordless walk through a meadow that seemed to go on forever. Milton would sometimes point out an oak that was particularly gnarled, and Heather would sometimes stop to point out a patch of cattails that was particularly wild, like a giant's uncombed hair; or they might both stop to examine the twist of wild wisteria branches, like long, bony fingers feeling their way up a yew trunk, holding it tight. But mostly, they simply walked, and listened to the swish of their steps in the dry oats and dockweed.

And when the breeze eddied just so, and they listened very close, they *both* heard the jangle of the bluebells, sprinkled on the wind.

EPILOGUE

LORIEN

Adrian Plackett never did put *Lorien* on display. Upon returning to London, he consigned the statue to his basement hoard, where it remained locked away. A pedestal he had created specifically for her was left empty.

When Lady Mariah and her kin descended upon him to hear about his expedition, he ordered them away. As he could not go anywhere without being asked questions, and as he so objected to the subject that it brought him to a boil, he made himself more scarce in the art-collecting circles, and eventually disappeared from them.

Shortly thereafter, he became ill.

Although no one could determine the cause of his illness, secretly his servants suspected it had something to do with abstinence from the art world that he had so doggedly pursued for years. He lay in bed for weeks, muttering to the empty walls, his eyelids fluttering like two wounded moth wings. He groaned for a doctor, so a doctor was summoned, who studied his eyes and ears and nose and coated lizard throat, then prescribed a quantity of this elixir and that tonic to be taken three times daily, along with a lot of rest. When these remedies proved ineffective, Adrian sent for another doctor who looked in the same places, and prescribed different quantities of different tonics and elixirs, along with a great deal more rest, all of which proved just as useless. So it went with a number of other doctors who all peered down the pale reptilian gullet of the incurable man, until he had dismissed them all with a cough and a sputter, resigned instead to sweating through his fevers on his own and teaching them all a lesson.

For the first time ever, the Plackett household fell calm. The harmony of the Diorama, albeit unsettled, for the first time went unchecked, and with no skirmishes to put down and no fires to put out, his servants hardly knew what to do. They waited on Adrian diligently, walking as if they balanced books on their heads, so slowly and cautiously did they move; and even when they met each other in some remote wing of the estate far from earshot of his room, they spoke in whispers, as though they feared the faintest sound might ripple through the chambers and awaken him.

Their fear was unwarranted. By rapid degrees, their master slipped deeper and deeper into his illness, until his head hardly showed above its waters. He stopped reading newspapers. He stopped reading books. He lost track of what hour it was, and didn't bother to ask. After a few months, he lost track of what day it was. All he knew was that the room was too hot, or too cold, or that his limbs ached, or that they felt numb, or that he needed food or liquid. As his condition worsened, even his appetite diminished.

His world had shrunk.

He became so ill that the care of Plackett Manor eventually fell to his butler, who had recently been promoted to that post from the previous position of footman, or Toy Soldier. He proved to be an able attendant of the Plackett Manor affairs, and even assumed responsibility for managing the estate's financial matters, upon which he discovered, without much surprise, that his master's exorbitant spending habits had driven him to the brink of calamitous debt. In an effort to remedy this, and without his master's approval (or disapproval, for Mr. Plackett was far too lost in the lakes of delirium to follow the Toy Soldier's affairs), he held an auction to liquidate the surplus collectibles that had accumulated in the basement, and thus save his master from debtor's prison, and the estate from ruin.

Among the pieces that escaped the basement was *Lorien*.

The statue made a brief appearance at the auction, which Lady Mariah and many others attended. It was purchased by an unknown man from Barnstaple, near its old home, and was never seen or heard of again.

A C K N O W L E D G M E N T S

We gratefully acknowledge the following sources for the interior illustrations of *Lorien Lost* as keyed here in italics to their page number within this novel:

Anonymous, *Roses and Holly: A Gift-Book for All the Year.* Edinburgh: William P. Nimmo, 1867. *8*

Bowles & Carver. *Old English Cuts and Illustrations for Artists and Craftspeople.* New York: Dover Publications, 1970. *85*

Downing, A. J. *The Architecture of Country Houses* (reprint of 1850 edition). New York: Dover Publications, 1969. *55, 163*

Eastlake, Charles L. *Hints on Household Taste* (reprint of 1878 edition). New York: Dover Publications, 1969. *68, 164*

George Bruce's Son and Co. *Victorian Frames, Border and Cuts* (selections from *Specimens of Printing Types*, 1882). New York: Dover Publications, 1976. *71, 191*

Grafton, Carol Belanger (editor). *Doré Spot Illustrations*. New York: Dover Publications, 1987. *82*

———. *Humorous Victorian Spot Illustrations.* New York: Dover Publications, 1985. *65*

———. *Pictorial Archive of Printer's Ornaments from the Renaissance to the 20th Century.* New York: Dover Publications, 1980. *39*

———. *2001 Decorative Cuts and Ornaments.* New York: Dover Publications, 1988. *192*

Harter, Jim (editor). *Animals.* New York: Dover Publications, 1979. *39*

———. *Food and Drink.* New York: Dover Publications, 1983. *154, 179, 181*

———. *Hands.* New York: Dover Publications, 1985. *130, 185, 188*

———. *Music.* New York: Dover Publications, 1980. *101, 166*

Heck, J. G. *Heck's Pictorial Archive of Nature and Science.* New York: Dover Publications, 1994. *78, 122, 123, 124, 167*

Johnson, Fridolf. *A Treasury of Bookplates.* New York: Dover Publications, 1977. All chapter opening ornaments.

Lawrence, Louis. *The Seasons.* Devon, England: Webb & Bower, 1981. *12, 121, 171*

Lee Valley Tools Ltd. *The Victorian Design Book* (reprint of 1904 edition). Canada: Lee Valley Tools Ltd., 1984. *91*

The Meridien Britannia Co. *The Meridien Britannia Silver-Plate Treasury: The Complete Catalog of 1886-7.* New York: Dover Publications, 1982. *20, 21, 35, 43, 114*

Mirken, Alan (editor). *1927 Edition of The Sears, Roebuck Catalogue.* New York: Bounty Books, 1970. *170*

Mitchell, Vance & Co. *Picture Book of Authentic Mid-Victorian Gas Lighting Fixtures* (c. 1876). New York: Dover Publications, 1984. *95*

Montgomery Ward & Co. *Catalogue and Buyers' Guide No. 57, Spring and Summer 1895.* New York: Dover Publications, 1969. *108, 131, 142*

Rowe, William (editor). *Goods and Merchandise.* New York: Dover Publications, 1982. *23, 30, 60, 117, 127, 136, 138, 147, 174*

Sears, Roebuck & Co. *Sears, Roebuck Home Builder's Catalog: The Complete Illustrated 1910 Edition.* New York: Dover Publications, 1990. *110*

Zucker, Irving (editor). *A Source Book of Advertising Art.* New York: Bonanza Books, 1964. *49, 160*

First-time novelist MICHAEL KING is a graphics designer who lives in Santa Cruz, California.

Chapters
Feb/98